*Matt pulled away slowly,
smiling as he gazed at the pleasure
evident in her face . . .*

Her echoing smile seemed to answer his unspoken question, for he returned his mouth to hers, this time with a subtle pressure, a vaguely sensual interrogation. His strong, long-fingered hands framed her face, the calloused thumbs softly stroking the smooth skin of her cheeks.

The roughness of his large hands raised silent questions in Jiggs's mind. Questions that would have shocked her sensible mind at any other time. How would it feel to have those hands on her breasts, her thighs? She drew in a breath sharply at the shaft of desire brought by her erotic thoughts. The breath she inhaled was Matt's and the intimacy of the action sent wildfire searing through her limbs.

WHAT ARE *LOVESWEPT* ROMANCES?

They are stories of true romance and touching emotion. We believe those two very important ingredients are constants in our highly sensual and very believable stories in the *LOVESWEPT* line. Our goal is to give you, the reader, stories of consistently high quality that may sometimes make you laugh, sometimes make you cry, but are always fresh and creative and contain many delightful surprises within their pages.

Most romance fans read an enormous number of books. Those they truly love, they keep. Others may be traded with friends and soon forgotten. We hope that each *LOVESWEPT* romance will be a treasure—a "keeper." We will always try to publish

LOVE STORIES YOU'LL NEVER FORGET
BY AUTHORS YOU'LL ALWAYS REMEMBER

The Editors

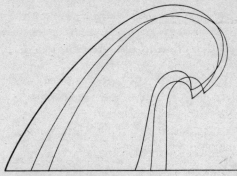

LOVESWEPT · 7

Billie Green

A Tryst With Mr. Lincoln?

BANTAM BOOKS · TORONTO · NEW YORK · LONDON · SYDNEY

To Dixie
She loved fiercely and was fiercely loved.

A TRYST WITH MR. LINCOLN?

A Bantam Book / June 1983

LOVESWEPT and the wave device are trademarks of
Bantam Books, Inc.

ISBN 0-553-21607-4

Published simultaneously in the United States and Canada

Bantam Books are published by Bantam Books, Inc. Its
trademark, consisting of the words "Bantam Books" and the
portrayal of a rooster, is Registered in U.S. Patent and Trademark Office and in other countries. Marca Registrada. Bantam
Books, Inc., 666 Fifth Avenue, New York, New York 10103.

PRINTED IN THE UNITED STATES OF AMERICA

O   0 9 8 7 6 5 4 3 2 1

One

"Oh my God!"

Needles of sunlight pierced Jiggs's tightly closed eyelids as shock held her body rigid beneath the covers. Very carefully she opened one eye, praying that she had been mistaken.

It was no mistake. There was very definitely a man in the bed! With both eyes opened wide in horror, she cautiously took in the broad expanse of bare chest beside her. She stared at the long, lean body as though mesmerized by the dark hair that curled down the middle of the bronzed chest, narrowed on the flat plain of the stomach, and disappeared into the blanket that was casually draped across the lean hips.

Her eyelids closed over confused, panic-stricken green eyes. What am I doing here? she wondered wildly. In her twenty-nine years of life, Jiggs had sometimes found herself in awkward situations. What woman hadn't? And she could usually rely on common sense and a deeply ingrained, natural dignity to carry her through the most embarrassing scene—but waking to find herself in bed with a total stranger was beyond her range of experience! There had been nothing in her life to establish a precedent for handling this type of thing. Promiscuity was foreign to her. It was a horror to her. It didn't fit into her well-ordered life. Jiggs was a neat, tidy person. Casual affairs were neither neat nor tidy.

So, what do I do now? she wondered silently. Her first inclination was to leave before the sleeping man beside her awoke. Never having considered herself a coward, she balked at not tackling a problem head on. But she had no recollection of this man and she didn't know how she was going to explain that diplomatically. The pounding in her head left her in no mood to cope with a wounded male ego.

"Good morning, Jiggs."

The deep male voice jerked her gaze upward to a smiling face set with laughing gray eyes. He had propped himself up on one elbow, dark brown hair falling forward across his forehead, and was watching her closely.

"Good morning . . . um . . ." She desperately searched her memory, but could not, for the life of her, come up with a name. Jiggs eyed his strong, unconventional features warily. Handsome was too tame a word to describe his face. No, not handsome, but breathtakingly striking—a stone sculpture before the rough edges had been polished away. His deep tan was not the smooth brown acquired lying on a beach, but spoke of long hours of hard work under the hot Texas sun. The whole effect was one of barely controlled barbarianism. She didn't trust him—not for a minute—but it was too late for second thoughts. She had obviously trusted him last night.

He stretched his muscular body contentedly, then dropped his eyes to her body above the blanket where a lacy strap had slipped off one white shoulder. After a brief, disconcerting moment, he looked into her confused eyes. "You don't look too pert this morning, darlin'." A secret amusement lurked around the corners of his eyes, but was quickly concealed as he said silkily, "You don't regret last night, do you?"

Regret what? she wondered, mortified, as she shrugged the camisole strap back in place. She had no idea what had taken place last night, but how do you tell a man that you can't remember his lovemaking? Oh, well, when in doubt—fake it. "No, of course not . . . um . . ." What in the world was the wretched man's name? "Of course, I don't regret it." Liar, she silently accused. "But I really must be going now." She kept her voice matter of fact and avoided his eyes. "I've got *so* much to do today."

"Why, Jiggs, I do believe you're shy." His hand came up to rub his jaw, effectively hiding a devilish grin. "You weren't shy last night, sweetheart. I'll never forget the way you seduced me with your willow-green eyes and tantalizing touch." His reminiscent smile had Jiggs gritting her teeth. "And the way you turned into a wildcat in my bed— biting and scratching while in the deep throes of passion." The strangling sound coming from Jiggs's throat stopped him for a moment and he looked at her with innocent eyes. "I beg your pardon? Did you say something? No? Now where was I? Oh, yes—the deep throes of passion. It was wonderful. It was good for you, too, wasn't it, Jiggs?"

"Well . . . actually . . ." She could no longer keep up the pretense. She simply wanted to go home and spend the rest of the day soaking away the pain in a hot tub. "The fact is . . ."

"Don't tell me you don't remember! Jiggs, you wound me." The accusation in his eyes was at odds with his strangely twitching lips. "You mean you don't remember the way you undressed me? You seemed very impatient."

"I undressed you?" she squeaked.

There was no doubt about it, the grin now appearing was very definitely wolfish. "Undressed me is putting it mildly. I should have said you ripped the clothes from my body." He gave her a knowing look. "You're so impetuous."

"Oh, no," she groaned, sliding lower in the bed.

"Oh, yes. Would you like to see what you did to my shirt?" He moved, as if to rise, and the blanket slipped precariously lower on his hips, revealing the drawstring waist of black silk pajamas resting indecently low on his hips.

"No, please." She squeezed her eyes shut in embarrassment. "I'll take your word for it. I'm sorry if I ruined your shirt. I can't understand it. Nothing you've told me makes sense. In fact, this whole situation makes no sense." Her earnest green eyes pleaded with him to understand. "I know this will seem difficult to believe, but I don't normally do this sort of thing. I'm totally, completely, painfully confused and I . . . I think I would like to go home now."

"But you can't leave now. Aren't you curious about last night? You can't leave everything up in the air." His long-fingered hand slid under the cover and rested on her warm thigh, his voice growing husky. "Maybe if we recreate the scene it will refresh your memory—kind of like an instant replay."

"No!" she said in a gasp, pushing his hand away. She began to sit up, then fell back with a groan, as pain pierced her temples. "I'll . . ." Her voice came out high, unnatural and she swallowed to begin again. "I'll probably remember the whole thing when the fog in my brain lifts." Jiggs felt lost and so vulnerable, a feeling that she hated. She gathered her strength and with a new firmness said, "May I have my clothes and privacy to dress, please?"

"I don't understand you," he complained in an exasperated tone. "You obviously came to my room expecting me to make love to you or you wouldn't have been in my bed when I arrived. So why play hard to get? Look, darlin' . . ." His voice softened as he swiftly, surely moved to half-cover her body with his own. "I'm sorry last night didn't turn out as you expected, but we can make up for it now," he whispered huskily, nuzzling the sensitive skin below her ear.

Jiggs stifled the unfamiliar shudder of pleasure that such intimate contact with his hard, masculine body sent rippling down her spine and focused her cloudy brain on his earlier statement. "In your bed? Didn't we arrive together? Weren't you at Max's party?" A nebulous memory floated through her mind. A crowded car. She was in someone's lap, fighting wandering hands. She winced as a stab of pain in her temples chased away the elusive visions.

"Jiggs, you don't have to pretend," he chided gently. "You weren't pretending last night. You wanted me and you came after me." He seemed not to notice her furious glare, his smug look congratulating her for her good taste. "I don't know anything about a party. I only know that when I saw you snuggled up on my bed, waiting for me, I didn't care where you had come from." His admiring gaze slipped from her face to her partially concealed body below. "You don't question a gift from the gods."

Jiggs's anger was lost in her growing confusion. What was he saying? If he hadn't brought her here, how did she come to be in his room? In his bed? She tried to give her voice a semblance of dignity as she asked, "If we didn't arrive together, when did I get here? Was I alone? When did you get here?" A note of hysteria crept into her voice as she realized how little she knew about the night before. "And where in the hell are we anyway?"

"You're serious, aren't you?" he said, studying her flushed features intently. "You really don't know how you got here?" She moaned in frustration, giving her head a short, negative shake. "Look," he said, his voice now firm and efficient. "I'm going to get dressed. While I'm in the bathroom, try to organize your thoughts, then we'll see if we can piece together what happened."

From his manner, Jiggs gathered that he was used to dealing with problems, and dealing with them promptly. The change was so remarkable, she simply stared in fascinated silence. As he finished speaking, he sat up abruptly and she nervously shifted her eyes to the ceiling.

Upon hearing the door close, she scrambled from the bed and surveyed the large room for her things. She found them lying neatly on a chair in the corner and hurriedly slid into the crepe de chine dress. A grimace marred her features as she caught sight of herself in the dresser mirror. The low-cut, midnight blue dress looked out of place in the brilliant light of day—it was clearly a dress for the soft lights of evening. Maybe there was a back way by which she could escape unseen. She looked anxiously about the room for a clue to her whereabouts. That she was in a hotel room was evident, but which hotel? The beautifully reproduced eighteenth-century Georgian furniture and plush carpet gave the room a look of subdued elegance. She mentally complimented the decorator who had echoed the room's chocolate brown and navy blue color scheme in the delicate pattern of the cream colored wallpaper. This was obviously one of Dallas's better hotels. She moved to the large window and pulled the drapes aside. In the distance, she could see the unmistakable shape of Reunion Tower, but before she could get her bearings, she heard the bathroom door open and she knew she was no longer alone. Jiggs turned cautiously to face him, feeling uncharacteristically shy. She had never been in a situation where she felt less sure of herself. She didn't like the feeling of having no control over her life.

His deep voice jolted her from her depressing reverie. "Come over here and sit down, Jiggs," he commanded, his voice brisk. "Just relax. We'll get to the bottom of this. I'm sure there is a very simple explanation."

She hovered nervously beside one of the brown velvet chairs before sinking abruptly into it as he gave her an impatient glance.

Lowering himself into the matching chair, he shifted slightly to face her. "Now, tell me just exactly what you *do* remember about last night."

She blinked in annoyance at his curtness, but swallowed a sharp retort as she realized that someone had to take charge and her fuzzy memory ruled her out completely. The fire dwindled in her spring-green eyes and she said with relative composure, "Last night I went to a celebration party given by a friend."

"And the name of your friend?" he interrupted to ask.

"Max Bueller."

"How close a friend is he?" he queried, gazing at the navy carpet with studied indifference.

"What difference does it make?" Jiggs couldn't understand his line of questioning.

"It could make a lot of difference," he muttered obscurely. Catching her puzzled glance, he added hastily, "Who knows—you may be a thief. That would make Max an accessory."

"What are you talking about?" Somehow she had slipped through the looking glass. Nothing was real anymore. "Accessory to what?"

"That's what we're trying to find out," he said, infuriatingly patient. "Go on—was the party held here at the hotel?"

"No, it wasn't here—wherever 'here' is—it was at Max's townhouse in North Dallas."

" 'Here' is the Beresford House," he informed her.

"We're making progress. At least I know where I am. Now if I could just find out how I got here!" She sighed in despair. "I knew I shouldn't have drunk so much on an empty stomach. I skipped lunch yesterday and Max's gluttonous friends ate everything in sight before I even arrived." He seemed fascinated by her face, his steel-gray eyes glued to her thoughtful features as she continued to explain. "I rarely drink, but Max kept proposing toasts and it would have seemed churlish to refuse."

"You said it was a celebration. What were you celebrating?"

"Max's new assignment. He's a free-lance photographer and he's just been assigned to do a peace series. It means he'll be traveling all over the world. Naturally, he wanted to celebrate." She recalled the mischievous gleam in Max's eyes as he refilled her champagne glass again and again. "I suspect he was trying to get me drunk. It's just the kind of dumb joke Max enjoys." She stopped to massage her throbbing temples as though trying to force the elusive events of the night before to the surface. "I can remember checking my watch at ten-thirty and that's the last truly clear thing that I can recall."

"Clear? You can remember things that are not clear?" At her nod, he asked, "For instance?"

"I have a very hazy memory of being in a crowded car." She leaned her aching head on the high back of her chair for a moment, then jerked upright as she remembered something else. "Abraham Lincoln!"

"I beg your pardon?" He looked at Jiggs as though he expected her to start foaming at the mouth at any second.

Unaware of his astonishment, she leaned forward, triumphant at having recovered a bit of her missing past. "Someone—I can't remember who— told me that Abraham Lincoln wanted to see me. I recall being very impressed that such an important person had asked for me." It took a moment for what she had just said to get past the pain in her head and sink into her brain. "Abraham Lincoln?" she whispered, turning tear-filled eyes to the man beside her. "I'm crazy, aren't I? I thought *you* were, but it's really *me*," she murmured incoherently.

"Jiggs?"

The gentle concern in his voice was her undoing. It released a trail of tears that ran silently down her lovely, confused face. Then strong arms came around her, lifting her, and she was in his lap, being rocked like a baby. Jiggs leaned against his strength, resting her weary head on his shoulder and letting him rock away her fears.

"Thank you . . . um . . . I'm sorry, I don't know

your name." She glanced up at him and sniffed pathetically.

"You're quite welcome and my name is Matt." His encouraging smile, viewed from this close range, brought a strange feeling to the pit of Jiggs's stomach. He smoothed back the hair that had fallen across her forehead, apparently unaware that he still held her clasped to his chest. "Would you like to tell me what that was all about?"

"Don't you see," she asked miserably. "I wake up in bed with a strange man, foul creatures are playing the Anvil Chorus in my head, I find out I'm totally insane, and . . . and my hair's a mess," she finished on a wailing note and buried her face in his shirt.

"Matt?" The word was muffled against his broad shoulder, which was, unreasonably, shaking.

"Yes, Jiggs," he answered in a strangled voice.

"May I go to the ladies' room?"

Low, rich laughter burst forth and filled the room. She stared at his face in startled wonder, mesmerized by his laughing features.

"I'm sorry, Jiggs," he said, controlling his laughter with difficulty. "I've been a pig, haven't I? Badgering you when you don't feel well and I didn't even offer you the use of the bathroom. After all the champagne you had last night, you must be in agony. Honestly, I wasn't being sadistic—I just didn't think."

"Really, there's no need to go into detail." She turned her head and began to memorize the pattern in the wallpaper as crimson flooded her face. "May I go now?"

"Of course," he said, releasing her, then handing her the satin evening purse which had lain on the table between the chairs.

Realizing that he was barely suppressing his laughter, Jiggs hurried from the room in embarrassment. Minutes later as she surveyed her disheveled appearance in the bathroom mirror, she railed at the fates that had led her into this predicament. "When I get my hands on Max," she muttered, "he'll wish he had never heard of Jiggs O'Malley."

She pulled the comb viciously through her tangled auburn locks, viewing the results with displeasure. "Mirror, mirror . . . well, come on," she urged, "who's the fairest? Bo Derek?" She turned from the mirror in disgust and complained, "Don't you ever read fairy tales? That's all I need—an honest mirror." Directing a rude gesture at the unobliging mirror, she squared her shoulders, took a deep breath, and made up her mind to be out of the hotel and back in the real world as quickly as possible.

Matt was still sitting where she had left him. Like the Raven, "never flitting," she thought, then wondered if she was becoming hysterical again.

Sensing her presence, he turned his head and said, "Feeling better now, Jiggs?"

His hastily stifled grin had her mentally wincing, but she answered calmly, "I'm fine, thank you." She sat down in the chair she had vacated earlier and faced him with what she hoped was a dignified expression. "Matt, I've told you all I know about last night. Could you do the same? Leaving out the intimate details," she hurried to add. "Just tell me what you know about how I came to be in your room. Please."

"I honestly don't know how you got here, Jiggs," he answered seriously. "I returned to my room about twelve-thirty this morning and you were asleep on my bed."

"Asleep . . . on your bed. I see." She swallowed her mortification. "Then what?"

"Well, I wasn't bothered at first because I had

been expecting a visitor—her coloring is similar to yours." His swift examination of her body seemed to say it was the only similarity. "Once I had realized my mistake, I tried to wake you. You revived long enough to tell me your first name . . . and that I was cute. . . ." Jiggs shifted in embarrassment at his mocking glance. ". . . then you passed out cold, so I made you comfortable and let you sleep. I just assumed you were looking for a good time and had bribed someone to let you into my room."

She looked at him curiously. "Do women often bribe their way into your room?" His wicked grin brought an answering smile to her well-shaped lips. If you smile at them like that, she thought, I can't really blame them.

She glanced away from the distraction of his smile and began to concentrate on what he had told her about the night before. He said he had made her comfortable and let her sleep. Since she had been wearing only her camisole and panties when she woke up, Jiggs decided not to probe into *how* he had made her "comfortable." Suddenly, the gears in her foggy brain began slowly turning. "Matt, just now you said that you let me sleep, is that right?"

His outspread hands were joined to form a peak and he was whistling softly under his breath, carefully looking the other way. Finally, as if just hearing her words, he glanced at her. "What? Oh, yes. So I did."

"Then, all that business about my scratching and biting and . . ." her voice rose as her fury mounted, " . . . and ripping your clothes off. That was all a lie, wasn't it?"

"Do you know," he said, regarding her closely, "when you're angry, your eyes do the damnedest things."

"Matt!"

"No, honestly," he said, leaning closer. "They turn deep emerald green, but there are these crazy little flecks of gold that sparkle right next to your pupils. It's weird. Beautiful, but weird."

"Matt, why did you tell me those things?" she asked in exasperation. She knew she should be furious at his deception, but relief that she had not made love to a stranger outweighed her anger.

"I don't know. It seemed a good idea at the time. You were so certain that the worst had happened, I just hated to disappoint you."

His assumed innocence brought a reluctant smile to her face. "I'll accept that—for the moment—but why did you let me go on believing it?"

"Scout's honor, Jiggs," he said, raising his hand, "I thought that you had figured that part out yourself." His quizzical look seemed to question her intelligence. "You're not very experienced, are you, Jiggs?"

"I have been engaged," she defended herself heatedly. "And I really don't see that it's any of your business."

He conveniently ignored her irate comment. "You were so shocked at the idea of being carried away by passion and if the ex-fiancé didn't provoke that kind of reaction in you, then it's best that you broke it off." He gazed deeply into her eyes, as though he were trying to penetrate her very soul. "Because it's there, Jiggs, I can see it in your eyes."

His low, husky voice and sensuous gray eyes caused a tingling warmth to spread throughout her body. Her eyes dropped in uneasy tension to her clinched fists. He's right, she conceded silently. Roger's lovemaking had been "nice." And that insipid, unforgivably damning word applied to his personality as well. A nice, quiet, boring man who made love in a nice, quiet, boring way. However, she wasn't willing to discuss her limited sexual experience with Matt. Under normal circumstances, Jiggs would have given a bone-chilling reply to any such personal comment. But these were anything but normal circumstances. A more bizarre situation she had never encountered. The sooner she was out of it the better. She lifted her head, intercepting his thoughtful gaze. "Matt, you don't really think I'm a crook, do you?"

"Well . . ." At her sharp glance, he chuckled and continued, "No, I guess not. Why?"

"I just wanted to make sure before I leave."

"Leave! But we haven't had breakfast yet."

"No, really, Matt. I've got to go." She stood and looked down to brush an imaginary speck of dust from her dress. Now that it was time to leave, she felt awkward and strangely hesitant. She caught his movement in her peripheral vision and a moment later he was standing before her. His hand gently tilted her chin, forcing her to look up at him.

"But you're my guest, Jiggs, and I've given you a rough time. Let me make it up to you by giving you breakfast." The words were spoken softly, his breath a gently seductive caress on her face.

Jiggs shifted to move away from the disturbing closeness, only to find herself caught in the circle of his arms. She threw him an inquisitive look and was stunned by the desire burning deep in his gray eyes. She opened her mouth to deliver an indignant protest, but found his mouth eager to take advantage of her half-parted lips.

His fingers spread across her back and moved down her spine, smoothing the thin material of her dress over her curving buttocks, shaping her body against his. His hands skillfully caressed her hips before sliding over her stomach to her rounded breasts. Delicious shivers ran down her spine as he lowered his mouth to her neck, his firm lips and moist tongue teasing the sensitive skin.

The softly provocative exploration continued, spreading a warm languor through Jiggs's lower limbs. Without her volition, her body arched against his hardening length. He groaned deep in his throat at her response, intensifying his hungry caresses. "Your body is perfect, Jiggs." His voice was raspy, urgent. "Last night when I took off your dress and found you were only wearing those silly little pieces of lace underneath, it took all my willpower to stop myself from touching you. God," he breathed sharply, "I deserve a medal for that."

Jiggs caught her breath, shocked by the thought of him looking at her nearly naked body; then her brain, dulled by unfamiliar emotions, came to life as she felt him undo the hook at the back of her dress and begin to ease down her zipper. She knew that unless she took action soon, the situation was going to be totally out of control. Matt had an uncanny effect on her senses. If she stayed, her fears of sleeping with a stranger would become a reality. She had to find a way to divert his attention and make good her escape.

She brought her hands, which had somehow become entangled in his thick hair, down to push against his strong shoulders.

"Matt, wait." Her plea was lost against his lips as he once again sought the honey of her mouth. She pushed harder, her efforts meaningless against the concrete hardness of his muscular chest.

"Oh God, Jiggs, you're delicious," he moaned, his lips moving over the softness of her throat before sliding lower to encounter the rounded tops of her firm breasts.

"Matt—please!" She had to make him listen before she was lost in the enchantment of his touch. "Matt, you promised me breakfast."

Her words seemed to penetrate for he lifted his head and stared at her blankly. "Breakfast?" He shook his head as if to clear it. "You want breakfast . . . *now*?"

"Yes, please."

"I can't say much for your sense of timing, but I did make the offer. Okay, breakfast it is." He released her to run long fingers through his disheveled hair as though wondering what to do next, then turned toward the bed. "I'll have room service send something up. Would you like to see a menu?"

The moment he turned his back, Jiggs picked up her evening bag and headed for the door, the sound of her footsteps lost in the deep pile of the carpet. She was on her way out the door when he picked up the phone from the nightstand and glanced up to see her leaving. She slammed the door and ran, offering a prayer of thanks that the elevator was standing open at the end of the hall.

"Wait, please," she called as the doors began to close before she could reach them.

"Jiggs, damn it! Come back here!"

The doors slid silently together, shutting out Matt's face, red with fury, and Jiggs leaned against the wall for support, ignoring the speculative stares of the couple occupying the elevator.

As she walked from the hotel into the bright light of day, merging quickly with the crowd of uninterested pedestrians, it occurred to her that she would never see Matt again. Instead of being relieved, the thought unaccountably saddened her.

Two

Jiggs pushed through the sparkling glass doors of the new SPC Building, paused to get her bearings, then headed for the reception desk in the center of a forest of potted plants. At the direction of an efficient blonde, she took the elevator to the tenth floor, praying to the gods who govern such things that her interview would be successful. She didn't think she could stand another six months of photographing catalog items for McNabb's Pipe Company. Maybe it indicated a deficiency in her character, but couplings and cast iron elbows just didn't seem to inspire her.

On the tenth floor, Jiggs swiftly found Suite 1020 and after confirming her appointment, was asked to be seated by a plump, motherly brunette. The office was tastefully furnished in a quietly modern style, the cool blue and green color scheme soothing to Jiggs's frayed nerves. Through the glass wall she could see the sprawling city of Dallas with the familiar outline of Reunion Tower in the distance to her left.

Will I ever be able to look at that building without feeling embarrassment? she wondered, her thoughts returning for the umpteenth time to the events of five days ago. Jiggs deeply regretted the childish way she had handled her encounter with Matt. Running away solved nothing. She had not given him a chance to understand. He had, for the most part, seemed a reasonable man. He had also seemed an irresistible man, her good sense reminded her. No matter how much willpower she possessed, if he had set his mind on seducing her, his expertise and her weakened condition would have guaranteed his success. On the other hand, he might have understood her strong objection to casual affairs—if she had stayed long enough to explain.

Jiggs sighed deeply in exasperation. The same arguments had been swirling around in her head for nearly a week. It was no use crying over spilled milk—she would never see him again, so she might as well forget the whole episode. If you can, an unbidden thought silently mocked.

"Miss O'Malley."

"Yes?" Jiggs slid forward in the seat and looked at the secretary expectantly.

"Mr. Timms will see you now."

Jiggs stood, smoothing down her white pleated skirt and straightening her peach blazer before proceeding with outward confidence into the adjoining office.

She liked Samuel Timms on sight. He was short and bald and reminded her of the stuffed panda that had been her best friend at age five. Apologizing for keeping her waiting, he motioned for her to be seated.

As he went over the details of her resume, now

and then asking pertinent questions, he seemed gratifyingly impressed and Jiggs mentally crossed her fingers for luck.

"Miss O'Malley . . . may I call you Jiggs?" At her nod, he continued. "Jiggs, your photographic background is excellent." He paused to clear his throat, then excused himself to pour a glass of water. Apparently he was unaware of her growing tension. She sensed an imminent "however" and prepared herself for disappointment.

"As I was saying, I'm very impressed by your photographic background and although I'm not an expert, even I can see your pen and ink drawings are remarkably good. However . . ."

Aha! she thought, here it comes!

". . . as you know, there is one other requirement. This one has given us considerable difficulty. That is, it has eliminated quite a few otherwise excellent candidates." He eyed her with regret, as though mentally crossing her off the list. "I'm referring to the geologic background which we specified as a requirement for the position. I see that you had two years of geology in college. Have you had any practical experience?" He asked as though it would be more likely that she had been to the moon.

"If you mean, have I drilled any oil wells—then the answer is no. I spent three summers in the field with my paleontology professor, if that's any help." She forced herself to remain calm. Experience had taught her that it was bad strategy to appear overanxious.

"You've studied paleontology, also?"

"Yes. Under Professor Ian McKenzie—perhaps you've heard of him?" His enthusiastic nod of recognition gave her new hope. "I've done some drawings for the professor. If you would like to call him, I'm sure he would give you any information you need regarding my work." She leaned back in her chair and watched as he sat in deep thought, occasionally tapping his forehead with a pencil.

"It might work," he muttered, reaching for the telephone. "I hadn't dared hope for a paleontological background. Yes, it just might work." He seemed suddenly to recall her presence, for he replaced the phone and swung his chair around to face her.

"I'm very hopeful, Jiggs. But of course, you realize that mine is not the final decision." Her puzzled expression gave him his answer and he explained. "You will be working for Mr. Brady. That is, if he agrees, you'll be working for him and he will, naturally, have the final say. I'm Mr. Brady's assistant and it is my job to simplify things for him. It's a difficult job sometimes, Jiggs." He sighed deeply, then as if fearing he had been disloyal, he hurried to add, "Mr. Brady is a wonderful man to work for and I hold him in the highest esteem. However, at times, he tends to be what we used to call 'persnickity.' "

And obviously still do, Jiggs thought, suppressing a giggle and becoming more and more enamored of this man's gentle pomposity. But Mr. Brady sounded like an old grouch and she had to swallow her disappointment at not working for Mr. Timms.

"And Mr. Brady is? . . ." she asked.

"Why, he is the president of Southwest Products Corporation." His astonishment could not have been greater had she asked "Who is Ronald Reagan?"

"Mr. Brady is a geologist?"

"He *was* a paleontologist. He had barely begun his career when his father died, leaving him in charge of SPC."

"How could his father leave him the presidency

of a company?" Jiggs was becoming more and more confused. Corporate structure was just not her milieu.

"It's very simple," he replied. "His father was also the major stockholder."

"I see," she said, not seeing at all, but deeming further pursuit of the subject fruitless. "Mr. Timms, could you give me an idea of what's involved in this position? Mrs. Overby, from the employment agency, merely said an artist-photographer with a geologic background was required. She didn't go into it in any depth."

"Certainly, certainly," he agreed. "Mr. Brady is writing a book—or to be more accurate—recording a history. I know nothing of fossils, but according to experts, he has one of the finest private collections of trilobites in the country. You're familiar with this type of fossil?" She gave an affirmative nod and he continued. "During his years of collecting these fossils, he also collected some, as I understand, rather interesting theories on the evolution of the trilobite. His book will be a compilation of the evidence to prove these theories."

As he spoke, Mr. Timms's smoothly rounded face beamed with proud approval. If he inspired such emotions in this kindly man, Jiggs mused, maybe Mr. Brady wasn't all bad and, grouch or no grouch, the details of his work had her champing at the bit. She would give her eyeteeth to work on this project.

"I'll just give Mr. Brady a call and find out when it would be convenient for him to see you," Mr. Timms said, reaching for the telephone. He spoke briefly into the white instrument before asking Jiggs if three o'clock met with her approval. She nodded, trying to conceal her joy, and he concluded the arrangements, sending her on her way with his best wishes and an encouraging thumbs-up gesture.

As Jiggs left the building, she checked her watch and saw she had almost three hours to kill—plenty of time for lunch and browsing through the downtown shops, a treat she didn't often enjoy since McNabb's was located on the outskirts of town. She decided to browse first and wait until the rush was over to have lunch.

By one-thirty, as she stored her purchases in the trunk of her car, her stomach was rumbling in protest. She was only a block away from Jake's Grille, the tiny bar and grill that was a favorite of her photographer friends, so she headed for it, thinking longingly of Jake's frittata.

Inside she was greeted by several of her friends, urging her to join them at the curved wooden bar. Spying Max in the far corner of the room, she waved her regrets to her friends and headed purposefully for his booth.

"Jiggs, honey!" he exclaimed with delight as she halted beside him. "Where have you been? I haven't seen you since . . ."

"Since last Friday night, Max," she completed for him, annoyed accusation evident in her tone. "At your celebration party. I'd like to ask you a few questions about that party, Max."

"Sure, honey, sure," he replied, all affability. "Ask away."

Jiggs wasn't taken in by his agreeable manner. Behind Max's blond good looks lurked the heart of a fiend. He knew she was gunning for him and hoped to bluff his way out of it. "I'm not going to say anything about your prolific toasting on Friday night, Max. I figure I'm old enough to watch out for myself. However . . ." She gave a stern look. ". . . I do want to know how I got separated from the rest of the party."

"You mean you don't remember?" His innocent expression was ruined by the grin he was struggling to suppress. "What's the matter, Jiggs, did you drink too much?"

"You know damn well I did, you traitor. Now tell me what happened." She couldn't stay angry with Max. Her sober image had been a challenge he simply couldn't resist and he had had no way of knowing what the consequences of her drinking on an empty stomach would be.

"What's the last thing you remember, sugar?" he asked, realizing she was serious in her request.

"I seem to recall being stuffed in a car on top of an octopus, but the whole thing is very fuzzy."

"That was George. You know he's always fancied you," he explained. His blue eyes sparkled and he was no longer trying to hide his grin.

"George!" Her outraged expression was almost comical. "You know I can't stand George—why did you let me sit in his lap?" The thought of that middleaged Romeo's hands on her body made her shudder in revulsion.

"And how was I supposed to stop you, Ms. Independence?"

"You might have tried using a sledge hammer on George," she muttered darkly. "Okay, I know—you didn't take me to raise, but after practically pouring your cheap champagne down my throat, you could have at least kept George away from me."

"I resent your insinuations about the quality of my champagne." He looked at her with injured dignity. "Do you think I would serve my friends anything but the best? That was vintage stuff."

"I don't care if it was *Dom Perignon*. It gave me a headache that lasted three days—*three days*, Max!" Her green eyes flared as he tried unsuccessfully to hide a gleeful grin. "It also left a big, black hole where Friday is supposed to be." She pinned him with a determined gaze. "Now tell why I was in a car in the first place. Where were we going?"

Max appeared not at all upset by her tirade. He settled back on the black vinyl bench seat, stretching his long, thin legs out in front of him with an air of calm deliberation. "We ran out of champagne," he explained, as if it were an obvious conclusion.

Jiggs closed her eyes in frustration. "For heaven's sake, Max. How many people does it take to fetch champagne?"

"We decided it would be better if we moved the party to a place where there was an adequate supply of booze—so we went to the Miranda Room."

Resigned comprehension dawned in her pale green eyes. "Isn't the Miranda Room in—"

"The Beresford House?" he interrupted, his sharp gaze spotting her discomfort. He drew himself upright and looked at her intently. "Yes, it is. Why?"

Jiggs knew she would have to act for all she was worth in order to throw Max off the scent. His enjoyment of her adventures while under the influence would be magnified a hundredfold if he found out about her night in Matt's bed. Jiggs had a reputation for being numb from the neck down and Max would take wicked delight in debunking that myth publicly.

She mentally girded her loins and looked straight into his suspicious blue eyes. "I just can't recall ever having been there," she said casually. "When did I leave the party, Max?"

He stared at her as though trying to divine her thoughts, then shrugged. "I noticed you were missing around midnight. George said you had gone to the ladies' room. I figured you had given him the slip and gone home."

The arrival of the waitress halted further conversation, much to Jiggs's relief. She wasn't prepared to answer any questions about how and when she got home.

After they had placed their orders, Max excused himself to talk with friends on the other side of the room, leaving her alone with her thoughts. Her presence in the Beresford House was no longer a mystery. But why had she gone to Matt's room? And how did that ridiculous memory of Abraham Lincoln fit into the puzzle? It seemed more than likely that she would never find out. Oh, well, she thought, some people see pink elephants—I see Honest Abe. This rationalization helped to restore her sense of humor, but did nothing to satisfy her curiosity.

After lunch, Jiggs told Max about her interview with Mr. Timms and of the coming interview with Mr. Brady. Max knew of her passion for fossils and responded with optimistic enthusiasm. He could be a genuinely nice man—when his weird sense of humor wasn't leading him astray.

He finished his coffee and stubbed out his cigarette, his sharp eyes searching her face quizzically. "I could never understand why you took that stupid job in the first place. I mean, really, sugar— McNabb's Pipe Company?" He looked as if the words left a bad taste in his mouth. "You might just as well have taken a job as counter clerk at the local dry cleaner's."

While secretly agreeing with his statement, she felt compelled to defend her choice. "It hasn't been a bad job, Max. I work with some very nice people."

"Nice people! Lord love us, Jiggs," he said, disgust evident in his tone. "Honey, you've got a talent that most people would give their right arm for. And you sit there mouthing platitudes about the 'nice people' you work with—at a pipe factory! It's a damned waste."

Max was on his soapbox with a vengeance, the muscles in his thin, angular face contracting in determination. The subject was a familiar point of contention between them. Her refusal to see things his way infuriated and frustrated him. His eyes were beaming wrathful fury as he continued to rail. "It's more than that—it's a sin, Jiggs." As usual, Max worked his way around anger and tried wheedling. "Look, sweetheart, why don't you let me arrange a showing of your watercolors? I told Barney about them and he said he would look them over as a favor to me." The kindling fire in her now jade green eyes warned Max to back off. "Come on, Jiggs, I know you told me you didn't want a showing. But are you being fair to yourself? To the world?"

Jiggs clamped down on her fury and managed to speak with near civility. "You had no business discussing those watercolors with anyone, Max. You wouldn't have known about them if you hadn't been snooping. Now, for the last time—listen carefully—I . . . do . . . not . . . want . . . a . . . showing." She said the words through clenched teeth. "I know the loss of my talent will be a devastating blow to the world, but believe me, the world will survive."

A quick glance at her watch confirmed that it was time for her to leave. "Max, let's not argue. I appreciate your concern and I'm glad you have faith in my ability—I value your opinion." His snort of disbelief brought a sympathetic smile to her lovely face. "Someday I'll paint a room full of watercolors and dedicate them all to you. But I'm simply not ready to expose my work to the public and even if I were, I wouldn't let you blackmail your friend into showing my work at his gallery. I have to make it on my own." Her eyes pleaded with him to understand and forgive her stubbornness. "Won't you wish me luck with the 'persnickity' Mr. Brady?"

"Sugar, eyes like yours should be available only with a prescription." He stared at her in bemusement, his voice soft, his crooked smile self-mocking. "Of course I wish you luck." He shook off his oddly wistful expression as he watched her rise to leave. "Speaking of Brady—did you get to the Mathew Brady exhibit at the museum? I looked for you on Saturday, but I must have missed you."

"I couldn't make it on Saturday. I was indisposed." Her green eyes dared him to comment. "I'm going to try to catch it next week on my lunch break. I hope it's not crowded." Jiggs had arranged to see a showing of the works of the famous Civil War photographer with a group of friends on the day after the party, but she had needed time to recover from her hangover—not to mention her encounter with Matt.

"It couldn't be more crowded than it was on Saturday. The bourgeoisie was there *en masse*," he informed her cynically, then hurriedly said good-bye when he was hailed by a very sexy blonde entering the room.

Jiggs was still pondering the intricacy of Max's character as she made her way back to the SPC Building. He delighted in teasing her, even embarrassing her. Yet on several occasions Max had tried to change their casually warm friendship into a more intimate one. And although she admired his talent and was very fond of him, Jiggs had never felt the curious tug of desire that was necessary for a physical relationship. Her engagement to Roger had taught her that much. When a red-faced Roger had stutteringly announced that he had fallen in love with his sister's best friend, Jiggs's only reaction, after a moment of pique, had been relief. The fact that she had felt no pain underlined how wrong the engagement had been. Roger couldn't hurt her because he had never touched her heart. She wondered now if she hadn't chosen him for that very fact. She knew he would never expose her vulnerability. Nice, safe Roger. She would never enter into that type of relationship again. In a way, she had used Roger. She had used him to stave off loneliness. Jiggs had considered his infrequent sexual demands as the price she had to pay for companionship. But Max was too much a man to settle for that type of lukewarm affair. He would demand more of Jiggs and perhaps she wasn't capable of more.

Unbidden, the memory of the overpowering desire she had felt while in Matt's arms filled her mind and raced through her body, chasing away all thought of Max and Roger, and effectively contradicting her doubts about her own sensuality. She was momentarily consumed by a yearning for something entirely beyond her ken. Consequently, she spent the remainder of her walk lecturing herself on the adolescence of daydreaming about a man she would never see again.

This time she was directed by the beautiful blonde in the potted forest to the twenty-first floor. That gave her eleven additional floors in which to mentally prepare herself for the coming interview.

It was two forty-five when she walked into the quietly elegant outer office of the president of SPC. Although she was early, the brisk, efficient secretary informed her that Mr. Brady was ready to see her.

The inner office appeared to be empty and Jiggs looked around in confusion. A moment later, her gaze was caught and held by the tall figure sitting on a brown leather couch, in the shadows, against one wall.

"Hello, Jiggs." The voice was deep. The voice was amused. The voice was Matt's.

Three

Jiggs leaned against the closed door, squeezed her eyes shut, and slowly exhaled the breath she had drawn in sharply on hearing Matt's voice.

"I should have known," she muttered under her breath. "First Otis decided to have my new Italian sandals for breakfast, then that awful lady at the sale—I swear I've seen her on Saturday Night Wrestling—attacked me because I picked up the hat she wanted for herself." She sighed fatalistically. "Of course, it's you. It had to be either you or the lady wrestler."

"Who is Otis?"

Jiggs opened her eyes to find Matt standing directly in front of her, staring with the awed fascination of a man discovering a heretofore unknown species. She let her eyes range over his full length. He was tall. When she wore heels, the added inches brought her eye level with most men, yet he seemed to tower over her.

"Otis is my neighbor's cat. I'm cat-sitting while

she's on vacation." Her close proximity to the man who had lately disrupted her thoughts with disturbing regularity caused Jiggs's heart to pound in her chest, the movement visible under the thin silk of her blouse, and she began to babble nervously. "The cat has problems—serious mental problems—but being catless myself, I'm in no position to give Joanie advice on cat-rearing." *Jiggs, you're making an absolute ass of yourself,* she silently berated, unable to stop the flow of words. "Joanie's my next door neighbor. She's a wonderful person, but so protective of Otis. She thinks he's perfect, but, let me tell you, that is one disturbed cat."

As she chattered inanely, one hand crept behind her back and searched frantically for the doorknob. "Well, Matt, it's been really lovely seeing you again." Her fingers grasped the elusive knob and turned it surreptitiously. "I guess I had better be going now. You must be terribly busy and—"

"Jiggs."

"I don't want to take up any more of your time, so—"

"Jiggs!"

"Yes, Matt," she sighed in resignation, seeing her chance of escaping humiliation go down the drain.

"I thought you wanted a job?" He asked the question seriously, but with an irritating twinkle in his gray eyes.

She stared at him dubiously. "You don't mean you would actually hire me?" She snorted inelegantly in self-disgust. "People don't hire raving maniacs. Haven't you been listening to me in the last few minutes?"

"Yes, I have. But I've also seen your drawings." He eyed her hopefully. "Do you . . . uh . . . *talk* while you're working?"

She suppressed a smile at his tactfully understated question. "Never."

"Well, then there's no problem." He sighed thankfully, motioned toward a chair, and walked to his own chair behind the gleaming mahogany desk. "Why don't you have a seat and we'll discuss the job."

He isn't going to mention it, she thought in amazement. He was apparently going to ignore their misadventure of the previous weekend and calmly discuss business. From the moment she had recognized his voice, she had been unconsciously preparing for battle, her slender body tensing in anticipation of the confrontation. And now he seemed to be willing to forget the way she had childishly run from his hotel room. After instantaneous, knee-weakening relief came a moment of pique. He was obviously no longer interested in her personally. That's fine, she told herself, lifting her chin with a hint of belligerence. That's exactly the way I want it.

"Just one question before we get started, Jiggs." Matt was shuffling through some papers on his desk and spoke casually.

"Yes, of course," she said in her most business-like voice.

He looked up and grinned, turning Jiggs's insides to gelatin. "Who got the hat?"

She stared at him blankly for a moment, then laughed. "She did, of course. Do I look stupid?" His curiosity put her at ease. "Besides, I don't wear hats. I was just browsing."

"I guess that's as good a way as any to excuse your cowardice." He was laughing with her, leaning back comfortably in his leather chair. Rays from the afternoon sun streamed through the glass wall behind him and gleamed along his craggy cheekbones, giving his tanned skin the look of sculptured bronze.

"Believe me, if you had seen this lady, you would have considered discretion the better part of valor, too."

"I believe you. Women at a sale scare the hell out of me." Matt paused and leaned forward to pick up a typewritten sheet of paper from his desk, then looked at her searchingly. "I've been looking through your resume, Jiggs, and I've spoken with Ian McKenzie about you. Ian's an old friend and I trust his judgment," he explained. "He absolutely sang your praises. He not only recommended your drawings, but also your dedication and reliability." He seemed puzzled by something, his stare causing her to shift uncomfortably. "You're now employed by McNabb's Pipe Company?"

"Yes, that's right."

"Why?"

"I beg your pardon?"

"Why are you doing work that uses none of the talent that you obviously possess?"

Twice in one day was too much for Jiggs. She was tired of defending the way she ran her life. She took a deep breath and answered angrily, her narrowed eyes sparking green fire and her sensuous lower lip protruding slightly with aggression. "Because I have this real nasty habit that I have to support. It's called eating. And the way I choose to support that habit is my own business. If you object, I suggest you hire me, then we'll both be satisfied."

"My, my. We're touchy, aren't we?"

"Yes, I'm touchy," she admitted. "But be fair. I didn't come in here criticizing you for running this place when you clearly would rather be digging for fossils." Her own audacity took her breath away, but she refused to back down.

"Okay, I give. You're absolutely right, it's none of my business. But just to set the record straight—I wasn't criticizing, I was curious." He smiled at her and asked, "Pax?"

I wonder if he's aware of the effect that smile has on women, she thought, then realized a man of his obvious experience would have to be aware and, most likely, would use it for his own purposes.

She saw that he was still waiting for her answer and hastily said, "Yes, of course. Matt—I'm sorry—Mr. Brady, have you definitely decided to hire me?"

"Matt's fine, Jiggs. And, yes, I've definitely decided. After talking with Sam Timms and Ian, then looking through your resume and drawings, there was no question about it."

The certainty in his voice sent pride racing through her veins like adrenaline. "Thank you," she murmured, inordinately pleased by the unexpected praise. "Could you tell me something about your work, Matt? From the little that Mr. Timms told me, it sounds fascinating."

Matt evidently sensed her enthusiasm was genuine for he began to speak of his work as one devotee to another. As he explained how he became interested in the fossil arthropods and his subsequent search for the cause of their evolution and eventual extinction, Jiggs felt she could listen to his beautifully timbred voice forever. He seemed to have accumulated an unending supply of anecdotes from his years as a working paleontologist. The foibles and frailties, including his own, of scientists on a dig delighted her and his sensitive recounting of the courage and kindness of the people he had met on his travels, brought a sheen of unshed tears to her eyes. She interrupted occasionally with what she hoped were intelligent questions, and Matt answered in depth, taking her knowledge of the subject for granted.

Finally, he sighed with regret as he consulted his watch. "I'm afraid I have another appointment in fifteen minutes and we haven't discussed the details of your work yet." He paused for a moment, then, as though coming to a decision, continued, inexplicably avoiding her eyes, "Would you like to see my collection?"

"Oh, yes, Matt!" she answered breathlessly. "When?"

"Now—I keep it on the top floor." He stood up, still looking carefully beyond her. "You can look at the fossils, read my notes, then when I finish here we'll straighten out all the details. Okay?"

"That sounds fine," she said quietly, his strange behavior bewildering her.

In the hall, Matt bypassed the public elevator to usher her into another which was ominously marked PRIVATE in large, bold letters. His curious silence was beginning to make Jiggs uneasy. The elevator opened onto an elegantly modern hallway. It looked like no laboratory or workroom that Jiggs had ever seen. It looked like . . .

She turned accusing eyes to Matt who was whistling nonchalantly as he picked up a stack of mail from a narrow ebony table set against the wall, and began to sift through it, confirming her suspicions. "Matt!"

"Be with you in just a second, Jiggs," he said, casually ignoring her indignation. "I've been waiting for this letter." He looked at her with assumed innocence and said kindly, "Why don't you go on into the living room while I take care of this."

She gritted her teeth, but went as directed through the wide archway. If I didn't want this job so badly, she fumed silently, I would tell Mr.

Matthew Brady to stuff it. Does he honestly think that I'm naïve enough to fall for that old etchings trick? She paused in her thoughts to chuckle as she realized she *had* fallen for it.

She glanced around, then stopped in her tracks. She stared, mesmerized by the spacious, light-filled room. It was artistically perfect. Everything in it was arranged for a precise balance of space and color. But the room was dead. She couldn't believe people were allowed to be human in it. How could you argue, cry, laugh, or simply be bone tired in a room that forbade it? She carefully examined the space to discover a cause for the curious sterility. As she ran her eyes over the plush, silver-gray carpet, the stark white walls, relieved only by the splashes of color in the geometric wall hangings, and the clean lines of the white, gray, and rust upholstered furniture, she came to the conclusion that it wasn't the fault of the decor. The room was perfect—too perfect. There was not even a plant in it to spoil the perfection by dropping an occasional dead leaf.

"Awful, isn't it?"

Jiggs was startled from her analysis by Matt's voice close behind her. She turned to see him eyeing the room with distaste. "No, it's not awful. It's just—just . . ."

"Awful," he finished for her.

She laughed, charmed by the frankness of his humor. "Yes, I guess it is pretty awful. Do you live here?"

"Only when I have to," he replied. "My real home is on the Brazos River west of here. I'll tell you about it later." He glanced at his watch. "Right now I'm late for an appointment, so let me show you where I keep my work."

She followed him down the hall and through a door at the end.

"It's all here." He indicated several work tables loaded with labeled fossils. "Make yourself at home and I'll be back around five-thirty to finish our discussion." He said these last words on his way out the door, giving Jiggs no chance to reply.

Obviously he's not going to hang around to seduce me, she thought, disgruntled, then hurriedly reassured herself that, of course, that's the way she wanted it.

She looked around the untidy room, wondering where to begin. Besides the tables, there were dozens of boxes stacked around the room. Picking up first one specimen, then another, she was soon totally absorbed in his work. Some of the fossils were rough, barely discernible in the rock that surrounded them, but many had been meticulously cleaned. The samples she examined ranged in size from less than an inch to eighteen inches and the variation in the features of each showed a similar wide range. As she picked up one piece of fossilized trilobite after another, she found no two alike. She recognized some of the types from her geology and paleontology classes. Most, however, were unfamiliar to her and she read the reports, which were filed under the label number, with an almost hungry relish. Time passed unnoticed as she pored over detailed, sometimes highly technical reports. Although she didn't understand all she read, enough of it was clear to make it fascinating for her.

She paused to stretch aching muscles, then stiffened as she felt a sudden tingling sensation on the back of her neck. Glancing hesitantly over her shoulder, she saw Matt leaning against the doorjamb. He had discarded his jacket and tie, his shirt lay open at the throat. His eyes dwelt an inordinate length of time on her mouth, narrowing briefly as she moistened her lips with her tongue in a quick, nervous gesture.

He moved into the room, breaking the tense silence as he spoke. "Well, what do you think . . . about my work?" He added the last words to answer her puzzled expression.

Jiggs gave a short, self-denigrating laugh. "That's like asking a three-year-old child with a crayon what she thinks of Picasso's paintings. From the parts that I was able to understand, I would say it's brilliant. And I'm thrilled to have even a small part in the project."

At her words, he shoved his hands in his pockets and glanced quickly out the window across the room. She was baffled by his behavior until it slowly dawned on her that he was actually embarrassed by her praise. He looked like a small boy who had just been kissed in front of a group of his friends—pleased, but trying desperately to hide that pleasure lest he be teased. The humanness of his reaction was endearing.

He shifted his position, giving her a wry look. "I wouldn't put you in the same class as a kid with a crayon, but thank you anyway for the kind words. I hope my colleagues agree with you."

He sounded as if there were a very small chance of that happening and Jiggs, knowing how slow the scientific community generally was in accepting any new theory, feared he was right.

She rose to replace the page she had been reading in his file, then turned as he said, "Come on, darlin', let's find a drink," and disappeared through the door. He moved with the restless grace of a caged lion. When she entered the large room seconds later, he was draining his glass. Judging by the bottle, he was showing great disrespect for a very fine Irish whiskey.

He caught her astonished look as he lowered

his glass and laughed heartily. "Don't look so dis-approving. I'm not a lush. I was just trying to wash away the taste of a phony, self-made, back-stabbing, good-ole-boy millionaire," he explained. " 'We'll make us a killin', I guaran-damn-tee ya', boy!' "

His mimicry was perfect and she burst out laughing. "Do you have to deal with many of them?"

"No, thank God. Sam handles most of them. This one was particularly persistent, but I'd go partners with a rattlesnake before I'd do business with him. He wasn't too pleased when I brought out a file showing the shady deals he's been in-volved in for the last ten years," Matt said mali-ciously, a reminiscent smile curving his well-shaped lips.

"Enjoyed it, did you?"

"Loved it. It was one of the highlights of my career as president of SPC. It almost made the whole thing worthwhile." A faint look of regret came into his gray eyes, then he shook it off and looked at her apologetically. "I haven't offered you a drink. What would you like?"

"Ginger ale is fine."

He grinned at her as she asked for the non-alcoholic drink. "Chicken?"

"Definitely," she admitted, accepting the glass from him. "I learned my lesson. Apparently my metabolism is not compatible with alcohol." Now that he had finally brought up that fatal evening, their relationship had progressed to the point where she could discuss it naturally, without embarrassment. She mentally applauded his di-plomacy.

Matt poured himself another drink and motioned her to the couch, then stretched out in the chair opposite with a relaxed sigh. "I'm sorry I was so late in getting back. I tried to get rid of Jackson early, but Lord, he was a tenacious bastard."

Jiggs glanced at her watch as he spoke and realized she had been so enthralled by his research she had failed to notice his tardiness. It was almost six-thirty. "I didn't mind. If you hadn't returned when you did, I probably would have stayed until hunger forced me out," she told him and smiled.

"Speaking of hunger, I skipped lunch today and I'm starving. I've asked Ruth to set another plate, so we can discuss your job over dinner." He moved to rise, but Jiggs's startled look stopped him.

"Ruth?"

"My housekeeper."

"Has she been here all afternoon?"

"Yes, she said she looked in on you once to see if you needed anything, but you were so absorbed in my notes she hated to interrupt you."

She couldn't believe that she hadn't heard the housekeeper. She had felt Matt's presence the moment he had walked into the room. For some reason, this fact disturbed her.

"Shall we go in to dinner now, Jiggs?"

"I really should get home, Matt. Couldn't you just outline what you need from me, then we could go into the details later?"

"I'd rather get it out of the way now," he insisted. "That way you can be thinking of the techniques you'll use and the materials you'll need."

His logic was hard to fight, but Jiggs felt a vague sense of uneasiness at the thought of spending the evening with Matt. "I understand, but I had made tentative plans for this evening," she lied.

"If they're tentative, then no one will be upset if you cancel, right?" How smoothly he rationalized.

His damned logic was beginning to irritate her

and from his smug look, Matt recognized her irritation. She fumed silently and was about to insist on leaving when his words startled her from her purpose. "I'm sorry, what did you say?"

"I asked if you wanted to know how you came to be in my room on Friday night?" The expression on his face held all the assurance—and satisfaction—of a poker player who has just laid down a winning hand.

Four

"You know how I got to your room?" she asked, her eyes widening with surprise at the bomb he had casually dropped.

"Yep. I sure do." He stood and replaced his glass on the sideboard, then walked toward the archway.

Scrambling to her feet, she hastily placed her glass beside his and followed him out the door. "How, Matt? How did I get in your room? I talked to Max and he told me how I got to the hotel, but no one saw me after midnight. How did I—oh!"

Her words halted as she ran into Matt's broad back. He had stopped abruptly and now turned to face her. "It's a long story, Jiggs, and I'll tell you all about it *after* dinner," he said, smiling triumphantly.

"That's pure, unmitigated blackmail," she fumed.

"Yeah. Sharp move on my part, don't you think?"

"Do you really want to know what I think?" she asked, her eyes daring him to answer in the affirmative.

"No," he stated unequivocally, grabbing her hand and pulling her behind him into a small dining room. Her pleated skirt flared in protest of his abrupt movement, momentarily exposing long, shapely legs. "Now sit down and I'll tell you what you're going to be doing for the next six months."

Before she could question his high-handed treatment, he introduced her to Ruth, his thin, plain-faced housekeeper, who was bringing in steaming bowls of delicious, homemade vegetable soup. Matt then began to tell Jiggs of the problems involved in the work she would be doing for him.

He talked steadily through the meal, pausing occasionally to concentrate on his food or to answer one of her many questions. His vitality seemed to fill the room, breathing life into the magazine-perfect setting.

"So, you see, you'll not only have to re-create each specimen, often from a very small piece of the actual creature, you'll also have to re-create an entire environment—the world as it existed when the creature lived," he summed up. "I want to show each developmentally important type of trilobite in its natural surroundings. I want the reader to see the influences that were at work hundreds of millions of years ago, during the time that each type lived. You'll have to show what the weather was, what predators were prevalent, and what types of food were available during each time period."

Matt placed his wine glass on the table with a sigh of repletion, then looked at her inquiringly. "How much notice do you have to give at McNabb's?"

"Two weeks is standard."

"That's perfect. That gives me enough time to arrange things on my end," he said, more to himself than to Jiggs. She could almost hear the gears in his brain shifting to high speed. "Moving the collection won't take long. I'll get someone on it first thing tomorrow. In two weeks I should have everything arranged so that Sam can take over SPC."

"We won't be working here?" she asked in puzzled apprehension.

"I'm sorry," he apologized, seeming to recall her presence. "I didn't tell you about the move, did I? We would never be able to get anything done here. I would be too convenient in a crisis. So I've decided to move everything to my home on the Brazos. It's just west of Mineral Wells, isolated enough to guarantee no interruptions, but close enough to civilization for Ruth to do her shopping."

"Ruth will be there, too?" she asked, trying, but failing miserably, to hide her relief. The rapport that she sensed between them was not enough to make her feel comfortable about spending six months in isolation with Matt. Ruth, taciturn though she might be, would keep the situation from seeming too intimate.

"Of course," he said, surprised. "Neither of us will have time for cooking or cleaning. Besides, if we had to depend on my cooking for sustenance, I'm afraid we'd both come down with ptomaine or botulism or something equally unpleasant. How about you?"

"I don't think anyone has actually died from my cooking, but I wouldn't guarantee it," she replied, echoing his grin. "I have a few special dishes that I do well, but you can live only so long on a diet of dill weed dip and strawberry mousse."

The laughter they shared at their own inadequacies filled Jiggs with a warmth she hadn't known since she was a child. If anyone had told her she would feel this empathy, this oneness, with a man she barely knew, she would have accused him of fantasizing. Jiggs had been on her own for a long time—since her parents died when she was eighteen—yet she had never before come across this particular phenomenon. Not that she didn't have friends. She did. Good, close friends. Friends she would trust with her life. But with Matt it was different. There was an indefinable quality in their relationship. A quality she had been too confused to recognize at their first meeting. Maybe it was the sense of humor, present in each, that was always ready, almost eager, to surface at any moment.

"You'll love my home, Jiggs." His words recalled her to the present. "Have you ever been in that area of Texas?"

"I've driven through Mineral Wells on my way to the Guadalupe Mountains, but I don't remember much about it except that the countryside was hilly—and very beautiful."

"I'm glad you think so. It's a rough sort of beauty that not everyone appreciates." He looked at her thoughtfully. "It won't inconvenience you to leave Dallas, will it? I'm afraid I just took it for granted that you knew we wouldn't be working here." His tone was apologetic.

"It won't be inconvenient," she assured him. Apparently he was unaware of what a prize this job was. Jiggs would pick up and move to the Transylvanian Alps if it meant working on his project. "As soon as Joanie comes back from vacation next week and takes custody of her neurotic cat, I'll be totally free of responsibilities."

"Good. That's settled then." His face showed pleased eagerness, as if he too were anxious to begin working on the project. He rose from the table in a swift, concise movement she was beginning to recognize as characteristic of all his actions, mental and physical. "I've asked Ruth to leave our coffee in the living room. I believe we have one other matter to discuss."

The mischievous gleam in his eyes reminded her of his promise to fill in the details that were missing from her memory of that night in his hotel room. As she preceded him, she was astonished that she could have forgotten it. His eloquence at dinner had held her spellbound, driven every other thought from her mind.

The drapes in the large room had been drawn against the darkness outside. Soft, subtle lighting and subdued background music gave the room an intimacy that had been lacking earlier.

Now that he had reminded her of his promise, curiosity and the memory of acute embarrassment warred within her breast, with curiosity gaining ground each passing second. She sat on the long couch, as she had before, and fidgeted impatiently as she waited for him to begin.

"How do you like your coffee, Jiggs?" he asked from his position at the sideboard as he poured two cups from a tall, sleek, silver coffee pot.

"Black, please." She paused. "Matt?"

"Surely you're not on a diet?"

"No, I just prefer it black," she answered patiently, then tried again. "Matt, you said—"

"Good," he interrupted—again. "Your figure's perfect just the way it is." He let his gaze drift slowly over her slim body. The intimate inspection couldn't have taken more than a few seconds, yet she felt stripped by the penetrating look. There was a gleam of remembrance in his gray eyes and she could feel a telltale warmth stealing into her cheeks. With his words and his actions he had effectively destroyed the camaraderie that had been steadily growing between them throughout the evening. She felt a curious anger at the loss.

Disconcerted, she rose swiftly from the couch and walked to stand before a painting she had missed in her earlier examination of the room. "This is . . . interesting. Did you choose it?"

"You've got to be kidding." He had followed her silently and was standing directly behind her when he answered. "The entire place was done by an up-and-coming young decorator. He was recommended by a friend."

She shifted slightly to escape his suffocating closeness, then leaned forward, tilting her head to look at the splotches of orange and black on the canvas. "What do you think the artist was trying to convey?"

"I think he was trying to convey incompetence," he replied with dry cynicism. "And he succeeded beautifully."

Jiggs's peal of laughter echoed through the large room. Once again his humor had, purposefully it seemed, put her at ease and she went willingly as he drew her to the couch, sitting beside her and indicating her cup on the glass coffee table.

"Why do you live here if you dislike it so much?" she asked, genuinely interested. A man of his means should be surrounded with things that pleased him.

"You've got to admit, it's convenient," he replied. "If this place were important to me, I would have chosen a decorator myself. But I use it only for entertaining and for sleeping. It goes with the job. And as I said, my real home is on the Brazos. It's a home, not a reasonable facsimile."

"I see," she said doubtfully, knowing that if she had the means at her fingertips, as he obviously did, she would not be able to rest until she had brought some life to this plastic palace.

He leaned forward to pick up his coffee cup and Jiggs decided, now that the wall of sexual tension was no longer stretched between them, that she would jump right in and force him to make good on his promise. She looked at him sternly, her set face demanding his full attention. "Matt?"

After a quick glance at her expression, he replaced his cup on the low table and replied with comically overdone docility, "Yes, Jiggs."

She chuckled at his absurdity, but refused to be diverted from her purpose. "*Now* will you explain about that night?"

"Of course, why didn't you ask sooner?" His innocent expression didn't fool her for a minute. He grinned at her mock-glare and continued, "Let me tell you a story, Jiggs." He leaned back and extended his long, muscular legs, the fabric of his charcoal gray slacks stretching tightly across his thighs. "Once upon a time in a faraway land called Dallas, there lived a handsome prince." Jiggs giggled delightedly, as he modestly fluttered his eyelashes. "The prince was going through some very hard times. He was being set upon by dragons and trolls and wicked—but eager—interior decorators. Forced to flee his castle by dropcloths and fabric swatches, he finally found a place to rest his weary head. It was a modest little country inn called the Beresford House."

"So that's why you were there!" she exclaimed, then at his quelling glance, she murmured, "Sorry."

"As I was saying before I was so rudely interrupted, the prince decided to take refuge at the Beresford. After a couple of days, he grew lonely and decided to ask a friend to join him in exile. The friend he had in mind was known by the prince for her deftness in soothing an aching brow. She was also known for her beauty and . . ." he paused dramatically, ". . . her flaming red hair."

"The visitor you were expecting when you returned and found me instead," she exclaimed.

"Brilliant deduction, Watson," he congratulated her sarcastically. "And her arrival, or rather her non-arrival, is the key to the whole mystery."

"Tell me," she begged impatiently.

"I was expecting Barbie at eleven-thirty, but had to go out at the last minute."

"Barbie?" she repeated, one arched eyebrow raised in malicious inquiry. "And you're her Ken?" she asked sweetly.

"Stop interrupting, cat. On my way out, I tipped the night clerk to watch for Barbie, take her to my room, and unlock the door for her. Now we come to the intriguing part. Enter Princess Jiggs O'Malley." He paused for effect, then resumed his tale. "The night clerk was waiting for a beautiful redhead to ask for my room number. When he saw a beautiful, but totally smashed, redhead standing in the lobby looking very confused, he assumed you were the correct redhead and let you into my room instead."

"You mean I just went meekly along to your room without asking any questions?" she asked in disbelief. "Even if I were a *little tipsy,*" she said, ignoring his raised eyebrow, "I would never go willingly to a strange man's hotel room."

"That's the weird part. Let me tell you exactly what the night clerk told me, then maybe you can make some kind of sense out of it."

"Yes, by all means, let's try to make sense, because frankly I don't believe a word of it," she muttered under her breath.

"He said he saw you standing in the lobby looking 'confused' and he rolled his eyes eloquently as he said it, so I assume he meant you were . . . uh . . . tipsy. He walked up to you and asked if you were going to see Mr. Brady, to which you replied with great perspicuity, 'Do what?' He said you looked at him as if he had a lot of gall to even speak to you. Of course, he said it in a much more picturesque way. 'Looked at me like I was a dead skunk' was the way he put it." He paused, then said admiringly, "The man truly had a way with words."

"Matt!"

"Be patient, I'm getting there. Anyway, he said he wasn't offended by your attitude because, even though you were looking down your adorable nose—my adjective, not his—at him, it reminded him of his daughter when she gets on her 'high horse.' So he repeated, 'Matthew Brady. Are you going to see Matthew Brady?' After a few minutes of deep thought, during which you stood there 'kinda wobblin',' you said, apparently very pleased with yourself for having found an answer to his question, 'Yes, I am. But that's tomorrow.' "

Matt looked at her inquiringly. "Did you plan on seeing someone named Brady on Saturday?"

"No, of course not," she denied emphatically. "The only thing I had planned for Saturday was to go to the museum with some friends. We were going to see the—" She stopped, struck, and whispered, "No. I don't believe it. It's too much."

"What? Come on, don't keep me in suspense. It's my mystery, too."

"We were going to see the Mathew Brady exhibit at the museum," she said in resignation.

Matt stared at her, puzzled, then after a moment of thoughtful silence, threw back his head and roared with laughter, ignoring Jiggs's sour look. She couldn't see that it was all that amusing. He was holding his sides, gasping for breath. When he finally calmed down, she was staring at him with an expression that would have been familiar to the night clerk at the Beresford.

"What's so damnably funny?" she asked in an icy voice.

He quickly smothered a lingering chuckle and said, "You won't believe it, Jiggs. You simply won't believe it."

"Try me."

"After you told the night clerk that you were going to see Mathew Brady on Saturday, he said, 'Mr. Brady wants to see you *now*.' He couldn't understand why you were so surprised!" Matt could no longer contain his laughter. His words were barely audible as his body shook with mirth. "Then you said—you said, 'Mathew Brady is *here*? In this hotel? And he wants to see *me*?'"

Jiggs's lips began to twitch uncontrollably and she burst out in delighted, unrestrained laughter. "I—I was in your room—" She spoke between gasps, holding her aching sides. "—I was in your room waiting to see a man who died in—in 1897!"

The look on her face set Matt off again. He pulled her into his arms and they rocked back and forth, tears streaming down Jiggs's face. "Not only that," he choked out. "You apparently expected Abraham Lincoln to be there, too!"

She let out another whoop of laughter. "Remember I told you I recalled something about Mr. Lincoln."

Matt leaned back against the couch, pulling her with him, bringing his laughter under control with difficulty. "The night clerk said you got 'real thoughty' in the elevator, then sort of wondered aloud if Mr. Lincoln would be there, too. He said you seemed 'kinda anxious' about it, so he assured you that if Mr. Lincoln was supposed to be there, he would be there. He gave me a very nasty look when I had to admit that you didn't get to meet Mr. Lincoln, after all. He was so concerned about you I didn't have the heart to tell him that you were referring to Abraham Lincoln."

"Oh, no!" She laughed. "I always associate

Mathew Brady with the portrait he did of Lincoln. That poor night clerk!"

"Poor night clerk, indeed! He accused me of luring you to my room with false promises." Matt's injured air didn't quite come off. "I'll never be able to set foot in that hotel again."

She looked into Matt's face. Tears of laughter had brought to her green eyes a sheen that evoked dew-covered grass, sparkling in the sun. "I'm sorry, Matt," she said contritely. "I feel like a fool. Are you sure you want to work with me?"

He seemed to make an effort to come back from someplace deep in her eyes and gave her a crooked grin. "Don't be ridiculous. Of course I do. And don't worry about my reputation. It will survive." He brought one finger to the tip of her nose in a soft, playful tap. "You saved me from boredom that night, because, if you remember, I was stood up."

Oh, yes, she thought, the brow-soothing Barbie. For some reason, Jiggs didn't want to dwell on her beautiful doppelganger's relationship with Matt. Her own relationship with him was baffling enough. He had merely looked at her earlier and her blood pressure had jumped sky high. Now, here she was, sitting cozily in the shelter of his arms, as much at ease as if she had known him—and his touch—for years. Apparently he could turn that sensually electrifying current off and on at will. A very convenient talent to have. A potentially dangerous talent as far as Jiggs was concerned. It could make living with him very uncomfortable, like living on the edge of a maelstrom, always wondering if today would be the day you'd be pulled into the strange vortex. Thank God for Ruth.

"Jiggs, darlin', am I boring you?"

His amused voice brought her out of her reverie

and she looked at him apologetically. "I'm sorry, Matt. What were you saying?"

"I asked if you ever managed to see the Brady exhibit?"

"No, I haven't yet. I'll probably go next week," she said. "Have you seen it?"

"Not this one. I saw the one at the Smithsonian a couple of weeks ago."

"The Smithsonian! Then this one will seem like small potatoes to you. I've read that there are more than fifteen thousand photographs in that collection. I'd love to see it." She sighed regretfully, then gave him an inquiring look. "Are you a photography buff?"

"No, not really. But since we do have a name in common, I naturally know a bit more about Brady and his works than the average person."

His hand, which had been resting loosely on her shoulder, moved beneath her hair and began a subtle caress on the nape of her neck. She could almost feel him pull the switch and release that exciting, slightly terrifying, current. He whispered words she couldn't hear as he lowered his head and placed soft, nibbling kisses on her earlobes, then her neck. The caressing hand stopped to push her long, auburn hair aside and he began to rain soft butterfly kisses on the nape of her neck.

Suddenly, her entire body seemed supersensitized—the soft lighting blinded her with its brilliance, the gentle strains of Chopin throbbed in her eardrums, and her clothes seemed strangely intrusive on her skin. Shock widened the pupils of her dazed eyes as her heart strove for a more conventional rate. With tenacious will she fought her way back to sanity. She blinked in confusion and tried to hear Matt's softly spoken words.

"Why did you run out on me, Jiggs?" He drew

back and, framing her face with his big, rough hands, looked into her troubled eyes. "Why?"

Jiggs's gaze dropped uncomfortably to the floor, then lifted to meet his puzzled look. "I'm sorry, Matt. It was childish of me." She murmured her apology earnestly. "I don't have a logical explanation. I simply couldn't cope. My resistance was low that morning and you were very . . . persuasive." She paused. "Running seemed the only solution at the time." His doubtful look forced her to continue. "I regretted it later. I wished that I had stayed and tried to explain how I felt."

"Explain now," he urged. "I want to know." He gave a short, harsh laugh. "Haven't you ever heard of the fragility of the male ego? I've struck out before, but I've never had anyone actually run from me. All week I've been wondering if there was something my best friends hadn't told me." He looked at her, his eyes commanding honesty, and asked again, "Why, Jiggs? I thought you felt the same attraction I felt."

"I did," she assured him, struggling to find the words to express her feelings. "I don't know how to explain without sounding like Goody Two-Shoes, but I'll try. I've been on my own for a long time, Matt. And I've been exposed to quite a bit of the so-called freedom that both sexes now enjoy. I made the singles' scene when I went through a depressingly typical stage of trying to be 'with it.' I've got to say it, Matt." She glanced at him quickly from the corner of her eye. "The truth is the whole thing stinks. When I went to those places with soft lights and loud music and wall-to-wall bodies on the make, I saw loneliness. A loneliness deeper and more desperate than any I ever felt sitting at home alone. I knew then—I guess I really always knew—that I wasn't the type to indulge in casual affairs. So many of the people I've met—not just in clubs, but at work, at parties, and even in grocery stores—seemed to be looking for something more than sex. They seemed, in some strange way, to be looking for themselves. It was as if they had to have someone near to confirm their own existence. Maybe it's some kind of big city syndrome. Whatever it is, I don't need it and I don't want it. I know I exist. I don't need that confirmed by anyone."

Matt leaned back, keeping his eyes on her face, listening to her words with deep concentration.

"I know what happened between us is not in the same category as a casual pick-up," she continued to explain. "We were victims of circumstance who happened to be attracted to each other. But, Matt . . ." She covered the hand that was resting on his thigh with her own. "If we had continued, it would have ended the same."

He turned his hand and captured her fingers. "What about your relationship with your ex-fiancé? Was it 'meaningful'?" His words didn't mock. He sounded as if he truly wanted to know.

"No. You were right about that." She stared thoughtfully at their entwined hands. "Roger was a sweet man, but I felt nothing for him physically. That was part of the lesson I've learned. I now know what I'm looking for. And someday I'll find it."

"And that is?" he asked, intercepting her gaze with a quizzical look as he brought her fingers to his lips in a gentle, non-threatening caress.

"I want a relationship that doesn't swamp my individuality. I don't want to be absorbed by any man. But then, I had that with Roger. So I know now that I also need to be attracted physically." She shifted sideways to face him as she warmed to her subject. "But even that's not enough. What I want is a man I truly like, that I feel comfortable with, but that I'm attracted to. I guess what I'm trying to say is that I want a loving friendship."

"Friendship? Is that really what you're looking for?"

"Yes. Don't you think that would be the ideal affair? I wouldn't have to worry if my hair frizzed or wonder if he thought my birthmark was ugly. Don't you see? He would be my friend, so he would care about the me inside the available body. I wouldn't hate myself the morning after and, best of all, he wouldn't tie my emotions up in knots because we would just be friends." She looked at Matt eagerly, wanting him to understand.

"Oh, I see all right." He laughed as if enjoying the antics of a child. "I'm afraid you're the one who doesn't see." He kissed the tip of her nose that had wrinkled in bewilderment at his statement. "Although you don't realize it, darlin', you just gave a pretty good description of love." He stifled her protest with a finger against her lips. "Oh, yes. Think about it a minute. You want someone who respects you enough to let you be yourself. Someone you enjoy being with, that you can laugh with. Someone who turns you on physically and who is turned on by you. And . . . you want someone that you can trust not to hurt you." He gave her a consoling grin. "That sounds suspiciously like love to me."

His words sank in and spread a numbness in her brain. Love? No, that wasn't what she wanted. She had miscalculated somewhere—or he had—but love was definitely not what she wanted! "No, you're wrong, Matt. There has to be some other way." Her words were urgent, almost pleading. "Surely a loving friendship is possible. I mean, sure, it's a kind of love, but not the 'till death do us part' kind. Right?"

"Hey, calm down. I was just teasing you." He pulled her against the comfort of his broad, hard chest. "Listen, baby, if that's what you want, then of course it's possible. There's nothing to be frightened of."

He tilted her chin so she was forced to look into his eyes. "What are you afraid of, Jiggs?" he asked in a gentle whisper, his voice gruff as if he were affected against his will by her fear.

A blush spread across her face as she realized how foolish her reaction had been. "I'm not afraid—not really. Your conclusion just took me by surprise, that's all. I thought I had the equation worked out so brilliantly. Then you came up with an entirely different solution." She looked at him in frustration. "It just threw me for a minute."

His look was frankly skeptical. "What have you got against love? I know some very nice people who are in love." He wasn't going to let it go and she silently cursed the way she had overreacted.

"Matt, don't be ridiculous. I don't have anything against love," she denied. "I fully intend to fall in love, and get married, and even have children—someday. I'm just not ready yet."

"Then why were you so emphatic about finding someone who wouldn't tie you down, wouldn't mess around with your emotions?"

"Because that kind of affair is sloppy! I lead a well-ordered life and that's the way I want to keep it," she defended heatedly. "The women I work with—married and single—come to work as if they are living on an emotional seesaw. One day they're euphoric because their love life is going well and the next day they're suicidal because it isn't."

"But haven't you ever wondered how that euphoria feels, Jiggs?" As she began an emphatic denial he interrupted her, leaning closer until she felt his breath, warm and smelling faintly of coffee, stirring the baby-fine curls at her temple. "I'm not talking about being in love, Jiggs, I'm talking about making love. Not the Milquetoast affair you had with Roger, but the kind of thing that makes you forget about your well-ordered life and simply feel."

He leisurely tilted her chin with one crooked finger and gently, slowly touched his lips to hers. The kiss was warm and soft and coffee-flavored. It didn't threaten. It didn't plead. It was a simple salute to her lips that brought with it a snug, sitting-in-front-of-an-open-fire coziness.

Matt withdrew slowly, smiling as he gazed at the pleasure evident in her face. Her echoing smile seemed to answer his unspoken question, for he returned his mouth to her lips, this time with a subtle pressure, a vaguely sensual interrogation. His strong, long-fingered hands framed her face, the calloused thumbs softly stroking the smooth skin of her cheeks.

The roughness of his large hands caused Jiggs to ask silent questions of her own. Questions that would have shocked her sensible mind at any other time. How would it feel to have those calloused hands on her breasts, her thighs? She drew in a breath sharply at the shaft of desire brought by her erotic thoughts. The breath she inhaled was Matt's and the intimacy of the action sent wildfire searing through her limbs.

Her parted lips were an invitation to plunder. An invitation Matt obviously had no intention of refusing. His hands moved to support the back of her head, his fingers becoming entangled in the rich silk of her auburn hair, as his coaxing tongue traced the outline of her lips, then slid with moist sweetness along the inner softness of her mouth.

Somehow all her nerve ends had become concentrated in her lips. They seemed alive with tingling sensation. His subtle exploration was a languid assault on her senses, a drugging adagio movement. Their bodies were not touching, yet she knew she was being seduced. She knew, but she no longer cared.

"You feel it now, don't you, Jiggs?" His whisper was simply an added caress, as was the male scent of him that invaded her nostrils.

She looked at his strong face with dazed eyes, knowing he had asked a question, yet unable to concentrate enough energy on her vocal cords to form the words to answer.

"God! You look drunk," he groaned huskily, triumphantly. "I knew it was there, inside you. And I want it, Jiggs. I want it all." He closed her eyelids over dilated pupils with urgent kisses.

Frustrated by his wandering kisses, she clasped his head fiercely between her hands and guided him to the aching throb of her lips. But the kiss was torturously short. She moaned in desperation as he pulled back from her lips.

"Is this what you need?" he rasped harshly, giving her another brief, hard kiss.

He was driving her mad. She was in a frenzy of longing for his lips. He had built a rapacious hunger inside her. Restless tremors shook her body as she pleaded, "Matt, please!"

"Oh God, yes!" His voice was unrecognizable, as if he were driven by the same demons that had taken over Jiggs's body—and her mind. He clasped her savagely to his chest, plunging his tongue deep into the ambrosial cavern of her mouth in an act as intimate, as possessive as the ultimate act of love.

The current flowing between them was intensified, surging and kindling a pulsating pressure in the center of her desire. In a convulsive movement entirely beyond her control, her agitated body arched against his, trying to assuage the paroxysms of desire.

In one swift, decisive movement, he removed her jacket, then eased her back until she lay beneath him on the couch. The feel of the hard, male body pressed against hers forced a groan of pure pagan delight from her throat.

Never had she received such pleasure from a man's body, felt such voluptuous satisfaction in simply being a woman. She felt a desperate need to celebrate her intoxicating discovery. She wanted to explore the cause of this tumultuous joy.

Cautiously, she removed her restless fingers from his neck and began light, searching strokes across his shoulders and, as he moved to give her adventurous hands free rein, over the muscles of his heaving chest. She could feel the intense heat of his body through his soft cotton shirt, but somehow it wasn't enough.

Jiggs lifted her eyes and found Matt avidly watching the hunger in her flushed features. As he captured her gaze, he began to unbutton her blouse in deliberately, maddeningly, slow movements. His eyes never left hers and his hand never faltered, even though the thin silk of her blouse was rising and falling with the increased rate of her breathing.

She closed her eyes and a tiny whimpering sound came from the back of her throat as he reverently touched her exposed flesh. She could feel her nipples hardening beneath the lace bra that was the only barrier between her and rapturously new sensations.

Matt's harshly drawn breath forced her eyes open. The wonder, the awe she saw etched in his craggy, tough face as he stared at her taut, erect nipples was a mirror image of her own. She gazed, hypnotized, as he released the front of her bra.

"Sweet, sweet Jiggs. This is what I ached for that night I held you in my arms." His voice was hoarse, raspy—a grating whisper, as he molded one full breast with his hand, cupping it to facilitate his greedy, sucking mouth. He drew the hardened tip deep within his mouth, his tongue taking and giving heady, sensual delight.

Her head thrashed from side to side, her hips arching against his throbbing maleness, and, from deep within her came a cry so barbaric, so basic, a saner Jiggs would have been appalled.

With the swiftness of lightning, Matt moved to capture the sound of her arousal with his mouth. The raging fury of the kiss did nothing to assuage their tormented desire.

In reckless haste, her wanton fingers unbuttoned his shirt and pushed it aside. Matt released her slowly from his frenzied kiss to watch her glazed eyes devour the rough beauty of his broad chest with its tight, hard male nipples. Jiggs was mesmerized, totally fascinated, and as though drawn by the force of a powerful magnet, she raised her head and, in a trance, slowly extended her tongue to caress the erect tip.

Suddenly, Matt was a madman. He threw back his head, his strong, masculine nostrils flaring, his breathing labored. He seized her to his heaving chest in a bone-crushing embrace. The mat of curling hair was an eagerly welcomed roughness against her erotically sensitized breasts. Her frenzied hands explored the rock hardness of his curved buttocks, his powerful thighs. She reveled

in the feel of his strength, the wonderful maleness of him. She wanted to feel that strength,
that masculinity against her bare skin.

His own hands had not been idle during her
exquisitely tactile exploration. She felt long fingers spread on her nylon-covered buttocks, cupping them and pressing her aching loins to the
matching ache in his. His hands were kneading,
molding, pushing down the offending pantyhose,
to feast on the rounded softness.

The movement of Jiggs's clumsy fingers searching for the buckle of Matt's belt brought her out of
her drugged state as effectively as ice water thrown
in her face. "My God!" she gasped, horrified. "What
on earth am I doing?"

She shivered spasmodically as shock spread
through her body. She had become a creature
unrecognizable to her sane, logical mind.

"What's wrong, sweetheart?" Matt looked at her,
concern in his sensually glazed eyes. "What is it,
Jiggs?"

How could she tell him? How could she come
this far and stop? "Oh, Matt," she moaned. "You're
going to hate me. And I don't blame you, I hate
myself." She sat up in disgust. "I'm no better
than a pubescent teenage tease. I don't know what
came over me. After all my fine talk about being
above casual sex, I practically ravage you on the
couch—a man I barely know! And then back out
at the last minute!" As she spoke, she furiously
jerked her clothing together, clasping her bra and
buttoning her blouse with savage gestures. "God!
I'm so ashamed of myself. Of all the stupid, ado-
lescent tricks. I'm supposed to be a mature adult
and I acted like an emotionally disturbed virgin!"

She slumped against the couch, her irrational
behavior defeating her, holding back tears that

would be the final humiliation. Staring at her nervously entwined fingers, she whispered miserably, "Aren't you going to say anything? Aren't you going to yell at me? Throw something?"

"Well, to tell you the truth, darlin' . . ." Amazingly, his voice sounded almost . . . amused. "I'm still recuperating from the shock. But don't let me stop you. You were doing a real fine job of yelling at yourself."

She lifted her gaze to confirm his mood. She was right. The now familiar twinkle was in his gray eyes, the crooked grin curving his strong lips.

"Matt," she said, bewildered. "How can you take what I did so lightly? It was unforgivable of me."

He put his arm around her in a reassuring hug and looked into her confused eyes. "Don't whip yourself, Jiggs. I was here on the couch with you. You didn't do anything alone. If anyone has to take the blame, then I should. I knew how you felt about it." He ran long fingers through his unruly hair and gave her a wry look. "To tell you the truth, I wasn't doing much thinking at the time. Things just got out of hand, darlin'. Can't we just leave it at that?"

"Yes, of course," she agreed slowly. "But even if you forgive me, I can't. I should have had more control. I can't understand what happened."

He chuckled devilishly. "Speaking as a totally unbiased observer—I was delighted with the way you lost control."

His delight was obvious—and expected, but Jiggs was definitely not delighted. On her second meeting with Matt, she had almost cast aside her hardearned reason, the well-ordered structure of her life. What was going to happen when they were thrown together for six months in the isolation of his Brazos home? She had depended on Ruth to counter the potential intimacy of the situation, but apparently the quiet housekeeper wasn't going to magically appear when Jiggs needed her.

"Don't worry about it, Jiggs."

Startled, she looked at him inquiringly and he explained, "You were worried about the next six months, weren't you? There's no need, sweet. I won't press you."

Her doubts about the future wouldn't be banished that easily and they showed in her expressive features.

"Look, Jiggs, remember what you said about wanting a loving friendship?" She nodded hesitantly, uneasily comprehending his train of thought. "Well, I think we've got the basis for that sort of relationship. But first, we've got to work on building a good, solid friendship." He chuckled wickedly. "I don't think we'll have much trouble with the loving part. We make magic together, darlin'."

Her face went beet red at his audacious observation. She struggled against her embarrassment and the fear that unreasonably overtook her at the thought of an intimate relationship with him. She needed time to think, time to make a rational decision about her future. Her recent brush with the sensual side of Matt had frightened her. Her logic, her sanity, had disappeared in his arms. Could she take a chance on being totally engulfed by an affair with him?

"Matt, do you really think it would work?" she asked doubtfully. "Earlier, you didn't seem too impressed with my formula for an ideal affair. Do you honestly think that type of relationship is possible?"

A strange, tender look came into his eyes. "As I said before—anything's possible if you want it badly enough." His smile was curiously determined as he repeated, almost to himself, *"Anything."*

He seemed to shake free of his odd spell and rose with her from the couch, helping her into her jacket. He turned her to face him, tilting her chin to smile into her still doubtful eyes. "Whatever happens in the future, darlin', I can promise you one thing. Our association will definitely be . . . interesting."

Five

Jiggs stepped from the small bathtub onto the white tiled floor under the inscrutable stare of a large brown cat and began to towel herself dry. Matt was due to arrive in thirty minutes, which didn't leave her much time for dawdling. He had insisted on taking her to the Mathew Brady exhibit and although she was still wary of the swiftness with which their relationship seemed to be progressing, she was too intrigued by the man and the way their personalities meshed to refuse his invitation.

"Well, Otis," she said, addressing the twitching leaves of a large fern on the floor which was the cat's observation post, "for good or for ill, I'm committed to working for the man. As for the rest, I've got two weeks to decide whether or not it's going to go any further."

Last night in Matt's penthouse when he had held her in his arms, she had lost the logic of which she was so proud—too proud according to some people. But the people who said that were usually men who were irritated because she had failed to fall in a heap at their feet. No, her logic and reasoning power were definitely not admired by men who were looking for an easy conquest!

But Matt had not been irritated by her reasoning. In fact, he had agreed to develop the relationship according to her rules. His attitude was a completely unknown quantity to Jiggs and the unknown was always a little frightening.

She was just stepping into the cocoa brown shoes which matched her moiré silk dress when she heard the doorbell ring, announcing Matt's arrival. Trying to slip on the remaining shoe, she hurried awkwardly across the room, tripping several times over Otis who was trying to claim another pair of shoes as his own.

"Otis! This pair is mine." Ignoring his hurt look, she opened the door to find Matt about to push the bell again.

She smiled, motioning for him to enter, but he wasn't looking at her. He was staring with wary fascination at the thirty pounds of fur disappearing beneath the loveseat.

"What in blazes was that?"

"*That* was Otis. It's one of his James Bond days. He's pretty harmless when he's playing spy," she assured him drily. "Just be glad you didn't come on one of his Bruce Lee days. I'm sure he thinks he's the reincarnation of that martial arts master. Anyway, his paws ought to be registered as lethal weapons."

"Aren't you afraid he'll pounce on you in your sleep some night?" he chuckled, watching the sinister twitching of the flounce around the bottom of the loveseat.

"Oh, he's done that already." She laughed. "I very nearly smothered to death before I got him off. Since then I've slept with my bedroom door locked."

Matt walked into the living room, looking around as he talked. "Locked? Surely closing it would be enough."

"You don't know Otis," she said ruefully. "Closed doors are child's play to him. I don't know how he does it, but I can put him out of the apartment so that he can play with dandelions or whatever it is that cats do for recreation and five minutes later he'll jump out of the closet at me. It's downright spooky, not to mention unnerving. The blasted cat has me so jumpy I've started knocking on the closet door before I open it."

"At least he's not dull." Matt laughed, then lifted her chin with one finger so that he could look into her eyes. "Hi, darlin'."

Watch it, Jiggs, she silently warned herself. It's a very bad sign when two softly spoken words can turn your insides to mush. "Hello, Matt," she replied in the same soft tone. "Are you sure you want to go to this exhibit? Won't it seem a little small townish after the one in Washington?"

"I wouldn't have asked you if I hadn't wanted to go," he assured her. "It may be smaller than the one at the Smithsonian, but that isn't necessarily bad. A small exhibit gives you more time to study each photograph."

"Yes, I suppose you're right. I would hate to rush through it, but I wouldn't want to miss anything either." She looked at him inquiringly, slightly ill at ease. "Would you like anything to drink before we leave? I don't have much, but I'm sure I could find something besides cooking sherry."

"No, thank you. I'm ready to leave if you are." He smiled indulgently at her nervousness and, calling a cheerful goodnight to the still-twitching fur, escorted her out the door.

On the drive to the small college museum, Matt spoke quietly about the Brady exhibit in Washington. His friendly, impersonal manner overcame Jiggs's attack of nerves and by the time they arrived she was once again looking forward to the evening.

On an easel in the lobby was a reproduction of the famous Brady photograph of Lincoln that was housed at the Library of Congress. It was a beautifully sensitive portrait that Jiggs couldn't view without a twinge of emotion.

She stared at the familiar portrait, feeling, as millions of others before her had, that she knew this man. The sensitive homeliness of his face, the hint of sadness in his eyes, brought an emotion closely resembling pain—a curious sense of loss.

"You really admire him, don't you?" Matt said, sounding surprised and a little touched.

"He was a great man," she said quietly.

"That depends on which history book you read," he said. "According to some experts he was an ordinary man who was made great by the unavoidable events which were taking place in the world around him. And some have even gone so far as to state that he badly mismanaged quite a few affairs while he was in office."

"I don't want to hear it," she protested. "Maybe I'm being naïve and unrealistic, but I don't want to hear that my heroes had feet of clay. I don't want to know if George Washington was fooling around on Martha. Or that Cleopatra was an ugly little broad with squinty eyes and bad teeth. Or that Abraham Lincoln was an ordinary man." She pointed to the portrait and said vehemently, "Look at that face. That is not the face of an ordinary man."

"Okay, okay," he said, laughing at her belligerent defense. "I don't know if I should be jealous of the man or grateful to him."

"Grateful?" she asked, smiling as she realized he had been teasing her.

"You went to my room last Friday night expecting to meet Abraham Lincoln," he explained, grinning. "You might not have gone if you hadn't been so impressed by him." He drew her arm through his and they walked into the first room of the exhibit. "I guess that makes me the only man alive today who's had Abe Lincoln fix him up with a date."

For the next two hours they were both absorbed by the photographs. Some were portraits of people who, though obscure today, had been the elite of that era. Some were poignant studies of soldiers in ill-fitting uniforms—heartbreakingly young men with confused eyes and rough, older men with sad eyes.

Matt seemed to sense when she needed silence to study a lonely soldier or when she needed to discuss a particularly interesting detail. She found his opinions and knowledge of history and photography as enthralling as she had found his anecdotes on paleontology. He was astonishingly well-informed on the events of the Civil War and they debated that tragic period as though it were a recent event.

When they left the exhibit they drove to a small neighborhood restaurant where their debates continued through dinner. Their enthusiastic discussion, which was interrupted periodically by their bursts of unrestrained laughter, drew indulgent looks from the other diners. But Matt and Jiggs were unaware of the presence of strangers. They were totally absorbed in each other. As much as she loved photography Jiggs knew that Matt would stand out in her memories of this evening.

They drove home in a comfortable silence, replete with good food and their own good company. How amazingly well their minds meshed! Although there were many things on which they disagreed, each sparked new ideas, fresh thought in the other.

Jiggs gazed out the window at the passing shadows, nervous anticipation building inside her. She couldn't let him leave without offering to make coffee and once inside, then what? Disappointment seeped into her mind as she felt the warm, comfortable companionship disappear, leaving tension in its place.

Why did she always anticipate problems? Why couldn't she take things as they came instead of making herself a nervous wreck over what *might* happen?

"You're mad about the cake, right?"

His voice breaking the silence brought her head around to look at him inquiringly. Feeling very foolish, she realized that they were parked in front of her apartment and he was studying her face intently. She laughed nervously and said, "I wasn't thinking about the cake, but if I had been thinking about it, I definitely would have been mad. It was outright thievery."

He stared at her tense features for a moment, then replied to her teasing words, overlooking her nervous tone. "I did it for you, darlin'. That cake was obviously too much for you to handle. You probably would have been sick if you had eaten it all." He looked at her, dramatically earnest. "So, with no thought of my personal safety, I finished yours as well as mine. You can see that I acted with the best of intentions."

Jiggs laughed softly, the tension draining from her body. "Your only intention was to stuff your face, Matt Brady," she said in mock indignation. "So you can cut the blarney."

He was still chuckling when he came around to open the door for her. "Being with you seems to improve my appetite for food . . ." He gave her a devilish glance as they walked up the stairs. ". . . As well."

When they reached her door she forced herself to sound casual when she turned to him and asked, "How about a cup of coffee, Matt?"

He gazed down at her, a crooked smile playing about his lips, and the silence stretched unbearably. Finally he chuckled softly. "No thank you, Jiggs. I'd better be going."

She stared at his face in the dim light, puzzled and a little chagrined by his refusal. Before she could frame a question he touched her cheek softly and said, "We're going to get to know each other, remember? It was very obvious that you were worrying about things going too far tonight and I'm afraid if I came in with you, you really might have something to worry about. There's a lot of electricity sparking between us, sweet, but I want you to feel right about it before we go any further. I decided last night to back off until you feel you're ready for the next step."

My God, she thought in astonishment. He can't be real. Nobody was that understanding. She was overwhelmed by his thoughtfulness. But how did one respond to that kind of generosity?

"Well?" he said, staring at her expectantly. At her quizzical look, he continued. "Aren't you going to save me from myself and talk me out of such a stupid decision?"

"No." She laughed, kissing his tanned cheek.

"I'm not and thank you for your understanding, Matt. You're a very unusual man."

"I'm going to take that as a compliment." He smiled ruefully. "Now before I go we need to talk about tomorrow."

"Tomorrow?"

"There's an open-air concert at Fair Park tomorrow night. How do you feel about Schubert?"

She hesitated for only a moment. "I love Schubert and I'd be happy to go with you."

He beamed his pleasure at her acceptance, reminding her again of a small boy, which was ridiculous considering his size. "That's great," he said enthusiastically. "I'll pick you up at seven and we'll grab a bite first."

"Why don't I fix something here?" she offered. "I have some TV dinners that I swear will fool you into thinking they're real food."

"You're on," he laughingly replied, then tilted her head and kissed her softly. "Shall I bring champagne, Jiggs? I have a terrible craving to see you the way you were last Friday night. So soft and cuddly in my bed."

A tingling warmth spread through her body at his soft words. "Maybe we had better go out to eat after all, Matt," she whispered. "I think it may be a while before I'm up to tackling either you or champagne."

Giving her hand a quick, hard squeeze he smiled gently and said, "I'll behave, I promise." He gave her a sly look. "Although the thought of you tackling me is definitely intriguing." With another fleeting kiss, he was gone.

She stayed outside her open door until she could no longer hear his softly whistled melody. It didn't strike her until later as she lay in bed that the tune he had been whistling was "Anticipation." Chuckling softly in the dark, she hugged her pillow, an inexplicable joy growing inside her.

The feeling stayed with her through her working day, bringing a smile to her lips at frequent, sometimes inappropriate times. She would suddenly find herself humming his softly whistled message as she worked.

On her way home from work she stopped by the supermarket to pick up the ingredients for a never-fail Mexican casserole, arriving at her apartment to find Joanie on her doorstep, eagerly waiting to claim Otis. Jiggs unlocked the door, juggling her groceries and trying to field Joanie's anxious questions.

"But did he eat enough, Jiggs?" the petite blonde asked, following her into the kitchen.

"Joanie, you worry too much about Otis. That cat is a survivor if I ever saw one," she drily assured her friend. "He ate all the cat food you left for him and two pairs of leather shoes. That should be enough to keep any cat healthy."

"Oh! Did he ruin your shoes? I thought I told you that you have to hide your shoes."

"No, you didn't mention it," Jiggs said, chuckling at Joanie's flustered look. "But even if you had it probably wouldn't have done any good. I'm convinced Otis would have found them wherever I hid them."

"He is awfully intelligent, isn't he?" Joanie said, lovingly indulgent. "Where is he, Jiggs? He usually comes when he hears my voice."

"Try the closet," Jiggs said, putting away her groceries. "But be careful, according to my calculations it's time for a Bruce Lee number. He hasn't been into martial arts for several days."

Moments later as she poured herself a glass of soda, she heard a faint voice from the bedroom.

"Jiggs, you weren't really partial to the green sandals, were you?"

Jiggs rolled her eyes in amused resignation. "No, Joanie. They were only an old pair. I had intended to throw them out anyway," she lied, then walked to the bedroom to watch the loving reunion—and guard her remaining shoes.

After Joanie had told Otis and Jiggs all about her trip to Canada, Jiggs reciprocated with a resume of recent events—leaving out the developing relationship between Matt and herself. Joanie was properly enthusiastic and promised to water her plants and watch for burglars while she was out of town.

Although she adored Joanie, she could see the minutes ticking away and was afraid that she was going to have to ask her outright to leave. Subtle hints went completely over Joanie's head, but as it turned out, there was no need because Joanie decided she couldn't wait a minute longer to give Otis the gifts she had bought for him in Canada.

Jiggs saw them out with a sigh of relief, then rushed around the kitchen, combining the casserole ingredients. When it was safely in the oven she quickly showered and slipped into forest green slacks and a cream silk blouse. She arranged her hair in a loose knot on top of her head, finally leaving the curls around her face and neck that were hard to be tamed. In a dim light, she decided she might pass for casually elegant.

The doorbell rang just as she finished tossing the salad. She ripped off her apron, trying futilely to smooth her hair as she walked across the living room. She was already opening the door when she realized she had forgotten her shoes.

Matt entered carrying a large bottle in a paper sack and Jiggs looked at him suspiciously. "Matt," she accused.

He grinned at her reaction and pulled the bottle out of the sack to show her the label. "Ginger ale," he said. "Now aren't you ashamed of yourself? Didn't I promise to behave?"

"Yes, you promised and no, I'm not ashamed. I don't trust you when you have that look in your eyes."

"Jiggs! I'm hurt." He sniffed the air, then followed the aroma into the small kitchen. "You're going to have to tell me what kind of TV dinner that is. It smells gorgeous."

"Actually," she confessed, "I was exaggerating slightly when I said I couldn't cook. If I have very detailed instructions and can throw out my first few attempts at a recipe, I eventually manage to produce something edible."

"How many times have you tried this one?" he asked cautiously.

She laughed, tempted to lie. "I've used it for years and no matter how I try I can't seem to mess it up. It always turns out great." Grabbing two potholders she took the casserole from the oven, carrying it carefully into the dining room with Matt trailing behind bringing the salad.

During dinner they talked about their respective days and as Jiggs listened to Matt's deep, beautiful voice, she found herself wishing they could skip the concert and remain where they were. But she knew that eventually the talk would dwindle and then that sizzling electric force would return to throw her into turmoil. So when Matt suggested it was time to leave she didn't demur.

The concert took place in the band shell at Fair Park and was exquisitely performed. They sat on the wooden seats, holding hands and letting the beauty of Schubert surround them. Afterward they walked through the park to his car, Matt's arm around Jiggs's waist and her head resting on his shoulder in contentment.

The following days were filled with excitement and laughter—and Matt. They explored obscure little art galleries and back street antique shops. Although they joined Matt's friends for an occasional evening, more often it was just the two of them. He seemed to take it for granted that they would spend every evening together and Jiggs was enjoying herself too much to object.

Toward the latter part of the second week Matt had to go out of town on business. Since he would be gone for several days they arranged to meet at his house on the Brazos and he gave her detailed instructions on how to get there. The evening of the day he left dragged on interminably for Jiggs. By nine o'clock she could stand it no longer and fled the too quiet apartment for the home of an artist friend.

As she rang the doorbell, the sound of loud music and voices filtered out to her. Jason, her friend, opened the door and Jiggs was hit full force by blasts of music, laughter and smoke-filled air.

"Jiggs! You're just in time. The party's in full swing now," he shouted cheerfully, then left her on her own as someone shouted for more food.

Although a mob scene wasn't what she had had in mind when she left her apartment, at least she was no longer alone with her thoughts. Across the room she spotted Max holding court and waved a greeting. She found a vacant corner when she saw him headed in her direction. He threaded his way slowly through the boisterous crowd, stopping every few minutes to give his opinion on whatever topic was under discussion in each cluster of people. He started a heated debate at each stop. Jiggs smiled. How Max loved stirring things up! He felt it was his duty to take a viewpoint that was in direct opposition to the one expressed. Consequently you never knew what real views he held.

He finally reached her side, leaning gracefully against the wall next to her. "Did you come to send me off on my adventure?"

"Is that what this is all about?" she asked, trying to make herself heard over the ear-splitting noise. "Jason left a message for me with Joanie yesterday, but she was so vague I couldn't make sense of it. I thought you had already had your celebration party. I dimly remember attending it," she added drily.

"I gave that one because I was happy to be going," he explained. "My friends are giving this one because they're happy to be rid of me."

She laughed softly at his cynicism, wondering briefly how much of it was real. "Who was the dark-haired beauty who was clinging to your arm with such fervor when I arrived?"

"Mandy?" he asked, after a moment's thought. "Mandy has been crossed in love. She gave her all—including the balance in her savings account— to her dearly beloved and he took a powder. Now she's seeking sympathy from anyone who cares to listen."

Jiggs grimaced in distaste. The idea of telling the world of one's humiliation was incomprehensible to her. How did supposedly intelligent women manage to land themselves in such ridiculous situations? Of course, she thought, there were no warning notices posted in advance that proclaimed a relationship might turn out badly. More than likely it started innocently and grew into something else. It could even start out as Jiggs and Matt's relationship had. How did she knew that she wouldn't be at a party sometime in the future, crying on the nearest shoulder?

Jiggs shuddered, horrified at the thought, then realized Max was watching her changing expression closely. He was the most unnerving man. . . . One always had the feeling that he was delving into private territory as he intently observed the world's antics.

"I think I'll go now, Max. If I don't see you before you leave, good luck and bon voyage," she said, hiding her disruptive thoughts as she stood on tiptoe to kiss his cheek.

He returned her friendly salute, holding her hand for a moment. "You take care, Jiggs. And if you ever need me, call my agent. He'll know where I am at any time."

She chuckled. "I can just see you flying back from Europe next time I lock my keys in the car."

"For that you can call a locksmith, but if you ever need a friend, you can call me."

But having a friend was what was causing all kinds of problems now, she thought as she drove home. What if her relationship with Matt turned into a sticky mess like that poor woman's? She was already very fond of Matt. How would she feel in six months?

The next few days were filled with turmoil, the nights filled with tossing and turning sleeplessness. She wanted to be with Matt and she wanted to be a part of his project, but she couldn't face the thought of their carefree friendship turning into something sordid and sloppy.

Headed west on Highway 80, Jiggs inhaled deeply. The first taste of fall was in the air, giving an added exhilaration to the drive. The breath-stealing heat of summer was beginning to fade, leaving a freshness that was all the more precious because spring and fall were so brief in Texas she sometimes felt she had imagined those mild seasons.

The change of seasons seemed to be echoed in the shifting tenor of Jiggs's life. She had almost driven herself crazy in the past few days, trying to decide what she wanted out of her relationship with Matt. Her only possible course of action had become clear late last night. Her friendship with Matt had to develop in its own way—in its own time. She was mature enough to handle whatever happened in the future and she had enough control over her emotions to keep from making a fool of herself.

As she drove through the gently rolling countryside, she congratulated herself on conquering her fear of an unknown situation. Reason and logic win again, she told herself smugly, forgetting all the doubts she had felt the last time she was with Matt.

Immediately to the east of Mineral Wells she entered rougher terrain—outlaw country of a century ago. The mesquite and gnarled cedar that grew in abundance appeared to challenge the right of the larger, more aristocratic oaks to grow in their territory. At one point, the road was cut through a hill of solid rock. The steep, weathered roadcut seemed to be a monument to the courage and determination of the people who had settled this ruggedly beautiful area.

Jiggs stopped for gas just inside the sprawling town and to reconfirm the directions Matt had given her. Then she continued west, passing over the winding Brazos River, and finally turned north onto a road of crushed sandstone which ran beside an ancient gas station made of native rock.

The crazy jigsaw pattern in the walls of the small structure was a reoccurring sight in this part of the country, along with piles and piles of cedar posts used in barbed wire fences.

She slowed her Pinto down to a snail's pace to cut down the clouds of choking dust that flew up from the narrow, rocky lane. Just as she began to think she was headed for nowhere, the road curved west and she began to catch glimpses of the river. Huge boulders shared the banks with towering cottonwood trees and the sparkling turquoise of the water was broken occasionally by a startlingly white sandbank. She couldn't imagine a more perfect place to spend the next few months. She would be right on hand when the leaves began to change color. Fresh air and the smell of burning wood would replace the gas fumes and pollution to which she was accustomed. My lungs probably will stop from shock, she thought.

She caught her breath sharply as she rounded another curve and was faced with the most enchanting house she had ever seen. It didn't jar the eye with startling beauty. It seemed a part of its surroundings—a brother to the very ground on which it stood. Made of the native Palo Pinto rock and weather-silvered cedar, the house appeared to have sprung from the earth, complete, without benefit of man's labor.

Jiggs pulled into the gravel drive, stepped from her car, and stood in silence. In the past, whenever she had tried to imagine the perfect house, only vague images had come to mind, yet she knew she would recognize that perfection if she ever saw it. And this was it. The kind of house that she instantly felt a part of. She let her eyes drift lovingly over the clean lines of the structure. It belonged to no architectural style that she recognized, but was in a class all its own.

Her gaze followed the deck around the corner of the house, then stopped suddenly as she saw Matt leaning against the rail watching her. He looked different. It didn't seem possible, but he looked bigger. She knew he was tall, but now he seemed a giant of a man, as if changing from a suit and tie to jeans and chambray shirt had given extra breadth to his shoulders, added iron to his thighs. An unexpected shiver shook her as he pushed away from the rail and moved toward her.

"Well, how do you like it?"

For one heartstopping moment she thought he was referring to her close examination of his body, then she realized he had meant the house. "Matt, it's lovely. It's the most perfect thing I've ever seen."

Jiggs almost laughed aloud at the apprehension she had felt in the last few days whenever she had thought of this man. How can you be afraid of a man who grins like an idiot when you compliment his house?

"I knew you'd like it," he said, his grin spreading, making deep grooves in his rough-hewn face. "Come on, let me show you around the inside. Then I want you to see the woods and the stretch of land along the river." As he talked, he grabbed her hand and pulled her behind him up the stairs to the deck, then through a beautifully carved door.

"Matt, wait." Sooner or later she was going to have to speak to him about his habit of pulling her around—preferably sooner before one arm became noticeably longer than the other. "Matt," she repeated as he continued walking, "what about my luggage? I'd like to change my clothes."

"Saul will take care of the luggage and what you're wearing is fine," he answered.

"Matt!"

He stopped and turned to face her. "Jiggs, I want to show you my home. You can change later." He looked at her quizzically. "Don't you want to see it?"

"Of course, I do. But first I'd like to freshen up." She wiggled her eyebrows at him to try and get the point across. "You know—*freshen up.*"

He stared at her eyebrows in confusion for a moment, then comprehension broke through. "Damn, I'm sorry, Jiggs. I did it again, didn't I? Just like at the hotel. I'm a terrible host. Come on, I'll show you your room first, okay?"

She sighed in relief and followed him into a large bedroom. The late afternoon sun, pouring through the windows, gave it a welcoming glow. It was a pale-blue gem of a room. The old-fashioned four-poster bed was covered with an exquisite crocheted bedspread. And a beautifully simple Quaker bench was placed beside a rocking chair in front of one large, blue-curtained window.

"It's beautiful, Matt. I can see why you're so proud of your home."

"You ain't seen nothin' yet," he boasted with a cocky grin. "I'll wait for you in the living room, Jiggs." He strode out the door saying, "Hurry. There's so much I want to show you."

Jiggs stood for a moment thinking about the complexity of Matt's nature. She had seen so many different facets to his character—shy and enthusiastic little boy, experienced lover, efficient businessman, dedicated scientist, and, briefly, totally enraged male. But she somehow felt she had yet to discover the real Matt. The driving force behind all his different faces. Did she really want to discover that Matt? If she found a vulnerability beneath his self-assured facade, wouldn't her own vulnerability respond?

She shook away the disconcerting thought and

went into the adjoining bath. When she reentered the bedroom, a very small, very old man was setting her suitcases beside the bed.

"You must be Saul," she said, remembering Matt's words.

"Yes, ma'am. Least I was last time I looked." He chuckled irresistibly at his own humor and Jiggs had to join him.

"I'm pleased to meet you, Saul. I'm Jiggs." She extended her hand to have it grasped in a gnarled, brown fist.

"Same here, Jiggs. You here to help Matthew with his book?" His voice was gravelly—the audible counterpart of his weathered face.

"I'll be doing the drawings and some photographs," she explained. "I'm really looking forward to working on the project."

"And so you should be. Matthew's a smart kid. I taught him everythin' he knows." The grizzled old man seemed to grow two feet taller in his pride.

"You taught him?"

"Sure did. Leastways, I taught him the important things. He went to college to learn about them giant bugs he's so crazy 'bout, but I taught him how to be a man. Did a damn good job, too." His faded blue eyes drifted around the room. "This house here—me and him built this house with our own hands and we didn't use no store-bought stuff either. We cut ever' stick of cedar and dug up ever' piece of rock that's in this place."

His eyes seemed to grow brighter as he pinned her with his gaze. "He coulda' lived in that fancy house in Dallas that his daddy left him when he passed on, but he didn't. He wanted a place that was his own. And this place—well, this place *is* Matthew. When you look at the rough rock in the fireplace and the weathered timber in the walls, you're lookin' at Matthew. Ain't no frills to that boy. He's rough, but he's natural. Ya' get my drift?"

Saul seemed to be giving her a warning of some sort, but why? Did he think she wanted artifice? She thought of Matt as he had looked when she arrived, leaning against the rail, wearing worn, comfortable clothes, and she could see that Saul was right. Matt had seemed a part of the house. She had seen him in a polished environment and, though he had looked polished also, there had been no pretensions about him. "Yes, Saul, I think I see what you mean," she murmured thoughtfully.

He grinned at her, showing a mouthful of surprisingly white teeth. "Good girl. Now you better scoot. Matthew's in there pacin' around like a caged-up bobcat." He chuckled. "Never could teach the boy patience."

She felt as though she had just passed some kind of test. But why should Saul feel it necessary to inspect her? Maybe he thought she would be a bad influence on "the boy." She giggled at the thought of Matt—forty at least, judging by the gray hair she had seen threading through the brown, and a six-foot mountain of a man—being called a boy. She certainly wasn't brave enough to try calling him that.

Jiggs quickly changed into a pair of jeans and a short-sleeved, green sweatshirt with "Frodo Lives" emblazoned across the front, then left to find Matt. He was standing in the large, open doorway of the living room, impatiently watching her traverse the hall.

"Come on, darlin'. Time's a'wastin'." He pulled her into the large living room, motioning about him with one hand as though introducing her to the room.

It was an airy, high-ceilinged room with one wall of that crazy jigsaw-patterned rock. In the center of the rock wall was the most enormous fireplace she had ever seen. It seemed to have stepped out of some medieval castle. Earthenware pottery containing plants and flowers was scattered about the room and the color scheme was taken from the huge Navajo rug in front of the hearth, with navy blue and burnt umber predominating. The room was more than homey, you could almost taste the welcome in it.

"I'm afraid my adjectives are limited, Matt," she apologized. "I can't keep saying 'It's beautiful. It's perfect,' but that's the way I feel."

He gave her a quick, enthusiastic hug and led her back into the hall saying, "I know what you mean. That's exactly how I feel every time I come home."

In the kitchen, Ruth was busy preparing dinner, so they only stayed long enough to glance around the large, efficient room with its gleaming white cabinets and huge wooden table that looked as though it had seen many years of use.

Matt led Jiggs through the screened back door and down the wooden steps. The area adjacent to the road had been partially cleared, but here wilderness reigned. It was cool and green and unrestrained. As they walked, Matt pointed out plants that were edible, including several types of wild berry, plants that were medicinal, plants that were poisonous, and some that were simply incredibly beautiful. His knowledge reminded Jiggs of Saul's words earlier.

"Matt, who is Saul?"

He leaned against an ancient pecan tree and nibbled thoughtfully on a stem of Johnson grass. "Saul? He's just Saul. There's no one word to identify him. He's friend, teacher, father, confidant, comrade-at-arms. He raised me and now he's my right arm. He's like this tree." He looked up into the huge, spreading branches. "He's always been here and he always will be."

Matt put his arm around her shoulders and they began to walk in silence. There were so many things she wanted to know. Why had Saul raised Matt instead of his parents? And why, if his father had owned a "fancy" house in Dallas, had Matt spent his boyhood here in the wilderness? But from Matt's silence, she gathered the subject was closed, so she turned her mind to the appreciation of her surroundings.

Suddenly, without any warning, they were standing on the edge of a cliff overlooking the river. In the distance to her right, she could see a massive sandbank parting the shallow, blue-green water, but directly below them it was deep and took on a darker, more mysterious hue.

For a moment neither spoke as they stood bound by awe of the natural beauty before them. Then Matt's voice broke the spell.

"How do you like my kingdom, Jiggs?"

She looked at the water, deep and dark beneath them, and, across the way, sparkling in the setting sun. "Anything I could say would seem inadequate, Matt. I don't see how you can bear to leave it for that plastic perfection in the SPC Building."

He hugged her to him, brushing the top of her head in a rough feline caress. "It gets harder and harder each time I have to, darlin'. One of these days I'm going to chuck it all and turn hermit." He tilted her head with one hand. "How about staying with me and being my hermitess?"

Although she knew he was teasing, Jiggs felt a shiver of yearning course through her body. Disconcerted, she broke the loose embrace and turned back the way they had come. "Shouldn't we be starting back? Ruth will want to serve dinner soon."

He followed close behind her, apparently accepting her abrupt change of subject. As they crossed a patch of rocky, open land, something scuttled across the dusty ground in front of Jiggs.

"My God! What was that?" she exclaimed, startled.

"It was just a little horny toad."

She looked at him in skeptical surprise. "I beg your pardon?"

Matt threw back his head and roared with laughter, the sound echoing through the surrounding trees. "I'm sorry. It's a horned toad," he chuckled. "We called them horny toads when we were kids—before we knew the word had another meaning. Actually it's not a toad at all. It's a lizard of the family Iguanidae."

"I don't care if it's a Rockefeller, it scared the hell out of me," she muttered darkly. "It looked like a Lilliputian dinosaur."

"You can rest easy—it only eats insects. They have never been known to attack lady artists—even terribly green lady artists. And even if one did attack, I would slay the fiend with my trusty sword. So stop worrying."

"Okay, Saint George," Jiggs answered, then suddenly began to giggle. "I can just see you with a huge sword, fighting that four-inch monstrosity. He would have to be a fire-breather to make it a fair fight."

"Well, he doesn't breath flames, but he does squirt blood if he's annoyed."

"Come on. I may be green, but I'm not that gullible."

"No, honest, he does. It's a kind of built-in protection, like a skunk's scent."

"That's grotesque!"

"Not really," he objected. "Every living creature has evolved some kind of protection. Sometimes it's obvious, like a porcupine's quills. Sometimes it's hidden, like the scent of a skunk or the blood of the horned toad. And sometimes it's a very subtle form of protection." He paused and looked into the woods behind them toward the spot where they had stood moments before. "Like the shell a human animal builds to keep from being hurt."

They walked the rest of the way in silence, each pursuing his own thoughts. Jiggs wondered if the easygoing charm that came so easily to Matt was a shell behind which he hid a more uncertain, less confident self. It didn't seem possible. He was always in control. Even when she had been carried away by passion, he had been in control of his emotions within moments of her withdrawal. Did he hide his deep feelings or did he have none? Somehow, remembering his boyish pride in his home and his work, she felt sure it was the former.

During dinner she watched him closely, trying to detect a crack, a flaw, in his attractive facade. As they sat in the dining room, which extended off the large living room, the shadows deepened in the woods and the moon rose, striking silver fire on the river as it wound around the wooded area behind the house, gently curving in to a sandy bank not a hundred yards from the glass wall through which they watched it. They talked softly of Matt's book and the plans Jiggs had made for her drawings and photographs.

It seemed to Jiggs that she had stepped into another world. It was not only the difference in the scenery or the freshness of the air. She felt as though she had somehow undergone a personal metamorphosis. She couldn't equate the way she felt now with the person she knew herself to be. She seemed to have left her orderly self behind, along with the heat and crowds of the city. The change made her uneasy. The tranquillity and contentment she felt here, with Matt, were an illusion that would disappear in six months when her job was finished. She had to remain objective and not fall any deeper under the spell of his magical kingdom. Her future sanity could very well depend on the amount of control she had over her emotions now.

"Have you come to a decision?"

His words broke through her intense concentration, startling her into awareness of his watching presence. "I'm sorry, Matt. What did you say?"

"I just wondered if you had reached a decision."

"About what?"

"I have no idea, but judging from your expressions, it must have been a serious one. For a while you seemed puzzled, then almost scared, then you got the most adorably pugnacious look on your face as though you had just decided on a course of action." He looked at her inquiringly. "You're not having second thoughts about leaving the bright lights and glamour of the big city behind, are you?"

"Bright lights keep me awake," she assured him, "and somehow glamour never decided to visit the side of town where I worked and lived. No, I'm not having second thoughts about that."

"About what then?"

"No second thoughts at all really. It just seems to me that it would be very easy to lose yourself, your goals, in this place. Things that were important yesterday don't seem as important today."

He looked at her thoughtfully. "Yes, you're right, but what you see as a threat, I see as a blessing," he murmured softly, almost to himself; then, in a swift change of mood, rose, pulling her to her feet. "Don't worry, darlin'. Jiggs O'Malley would be impossible to lose and if your goals are the right ones for you, they wouldn't stay lost for long."

Out on the wide deck, they had coffee in the moonlight and listened for a while to the frogs as they sang lovesongs in the night. The warm softness of the air enveloped Jiggs in a cocoon of sensual feeling. Oh, Lord, she silently moaned, I'm in trouble if the very air can seduce me. She felt as though her senses were being bombarded from all directions, bringing a fresh awareness, a rebirth. She had shed her old skin and this new skin was sensitive to every movement around her, every sound—the tiniest flutter of a leaf caused an echoing vibration to ripple through her body. She was in tune with the earth.

My God! she thought in horror, if he touches me now, I'll probably drag him off to my bedroom.

"Are you ready, Jiggs?"

Her face, mercifully obscured by the darkness, flamed and she sank lower in the wooden lounge chair. "I beg . . ." Her voice was a croaking mimicry of the frogs below. "I beg your pardon?"

"Now don't tell me you've forgotten. We're working on our friendship. Remember?" His voice held a warm amusement, as though he had somehow discerned her thoughts.

"Oh, yes," she sighed in relief. "Of course I remember."

"Good. A lot of it will come naturally since we'll be staying in the same house for the next few months, but to speed up the process, we'll play I love—I hate."

"I love—I hate? I've never heard of it."

"That's because I just made it up. Now be quiet while I explain. We each take turns listing the things we love, then the things we hate. And we can't include any big, universal loves or hates. We all hate hunger, war, and warts, so they don't count. Right?"

"Oh, I don't know about that. A well-placed wart is an inspiring thing. Can you imagine the Wicked Witch of the West without her warts? She would have been totally ineffective."

"Okay, I'll give you the warts, but you get my general drift." His appreciative grin added to the warmth of the evening. "You go first."

She sat thinking for a moment, then began. "I love Cary Grant and Jimmy Stewart movies; Walt Disney's animation; the smell of cottonwood trees; backpacking; English situation comedies; one-man-bands; cold buttermilk; John Philip Sousa and Johann Strauss—Junior and Senior; skiing; omelets in any way, shape, or form; bathing babies; chamber music; the Dallas skyline; old-fashioned hymns; and books—not just reading them, but the shape and feel of them. Now it's your turn."

"I love Texas at dawn; African sunsets; all music; murder mysteries; the smell of coffee perking; the sound of children—of any nationality—playing; Robert Burns's poetry; Saul's hands; Ruth's home-made peach cobbler—and watching you sleep."

"Disqualified!" she objected. "That last was a universal thing. My beauty while sleeping is legendary. It's only when I'm awake that people flee in horror."

"I'll concede your legendary beauty, but not the rest!" He chuckled. "Now your hates."

"I hate bubble gum, people who say 'You know what's wrong with you?;' flavored lipstick; jogging; frilly clothes; depressingly realistic novels; hamburger patties that you can see through; men who patronize; women who apologize for being women; arty movies; and mud wrestling." She looked at him inquiringly, enjoying the game.

"I hate the gritty taste of sand in dehydrated

eggs; people who tap you on the shoulder to make a point; wine snobbery; quiche; women who cry on cue; men who bully; people who ask 'What's your sign?;' and cold oatmeal."

"Apparently," she laughed, "you're a nicer person than I am. Your list of hates was shorter than mine." She glanced at him out of the corner of her eye. "By the way, what *is* your sign?"

"Slippery when wet," he replied. "What's yours?"

"Personally I've always fancied 'Piano for sale by owner with mahogany legs.' " she answered in the same serious tone.

"Now that we've gotten our signs out of the way, let's see what we've learned. I know that I must never tell you what I think is wrong with you and . . ."

"And I know never to tap you with my finger to help get a point across."

"And I promise," he vowed earnestly, "never to wear flavored lipstick or chew bubble gum when I kiss you."

"Right." She laughed, then sobered. "I do see what you're trying to do, Matt. But surely these are surface things. Do they really help us to get to know each other?"

"It's a start, darlin', and didn't you notice how many things we had in common?"

"Like what?"

"We both mentioned children, music, and literature as things we like. We both detest artificial, pushy people and we both like being outdoors."

"And I think I would have to agree with you on the cold oatmeal," she added.

"Wonderful! What a pair we make!"

"Matt?"

"Yes."

"Have you ever met anyone who actually *liked* cold oatmeal?"

"Sure," he answered, grinning. "My roommate in college loved it."

"Okay, you win," she laughingly conceded. "So we make a great pair. Now what?"

"Now we take it as it comes—go with the flow—do whatever comes naturally. I just want you to feel comfortable with me, darlin'."

"I want that, too, Matt. But you won't be angry if the other—the sexual relationship—doesn't evolve, will you?"

"Angry! Me?" he exclaimed, offended. "Upset . . . depressed . . . suicidal? Yes. But angry? Never."

"Oh, Matt," she reached across to where he sat and squeezed his hand, "I do like you."

He turned his hand, capturing her fingers, and stood, pulling her to her feet. With his hands resting softly on her hips, he pulled her forward to receive a gentle kiss. "Oh, Jiggs," he mimicked. "I do like you, too. Very much."

Later as she lay in bed, the warmth, the comfort of his kiss was still present and she prayed that if a loving friendship was indeed possible, she would find it with this man. She had kept such a tight rein on her emotions, she had forgotten what a wonderful thing true friendship was. It was a sharing that went beyond companionship. She hugged herself with the thought of, tomorrow, being able to explore Matt's kingdom and Matt's mind.

"What was I so worried about?" she asked aloud, laughing defiantly as the words echoed with a vaguely ominous hollowness throughout the darkened room.

Six

In the following days, Jiggs threw herself whole-heartedly into her job—and into her new-found friendship with Matt. In her enthusiasm she extended that friendship to include Saul and Ruth. Saul had sage advice and earthy witticisms to fit any occasion from brushing teeth to bearing children.

And Ruth's bland face hid a motherly soul that usually found expression in non-stop criticism. But even when she was scolding, neither scowl nor wrinkle marred her plain face. Her total lack of expression was a challenge Jiggs simply couldn't resist. Every time Ruth served a meal or passed her in the hall Jiggs had to restrain herself from making funny faces.

Finally she could hold back no longer. After Ruth had finished serving breakfast, Jiggs laid a hand on her thin arm to stop her from leaving. "Ruth, what do ducks who live beside nuclear laboratories say?"

Ruth looked at her for a moment, then said, "Well, Jiggs, I can't rightly tell, as I've never heard a duck actually 'say' anything, but I suppose that ducks being ducks wherever they live, would most likely make the same racket that God planned for all ducks to make. Of course, Mr. Johnson, my neighbor back home, had a duck that had been bit in the throat by a dog and it did make a kind of croaking sound. And some said it was talking, but the ones who said that were just as addled as that duck. Specially that old crone that lived down the road a piece. I remember the time that she—"

"Ruth," Jiggs interrupted, "this is a joke." She looked at the housekeeper in amused exasperation. "You're supposed to ask me what they say."

"Well, why didn't you say so, girl? I like a good joke as well as the next person. What do the ducks say?"

"Quark, quark." She looked at Ruth expectantly, but the older woman simply shook her head as if in pity and left the room mumbling about addled people. Jiggs stared after her in frustration, then turned to catch Matt looking insufferably smug.

"I could have told you that it wouldn't work," he chuckled. "Saul and I have been trying to get her to laugh, or even smile, for years. It can't be done."

"Well, you and Saul must not have been using the right ammunition," she said, more determined than ever. "That joke was probably too technical. Next time I'll try something more basic."

In the next few days Jiggs went from basic to downright corny. She popped out every time Ruth passed her studio, following the housekeeper down the hall with what was turning out to be a very bad monologue. To make matters worse, every time she tried, either Matt or Saul was lurking in the background to give her a superior "I told you so" look.

Finally, after the failure of her fail-proof gorilla imitation, Jiggs was forced to admit defeat. As consolation, Saul assured her that her gorilla act was one of the best he had ever seen and had certainly cracked him up. Although his words of comfort were appreciated, they couldn't drown out the sound of Matt's laughter as he leaned helplessly against his study door.

Saul looked at her, his expression serious, his eyes twinkling suspiciously. "And of course, you can see that the boy enjoyed it. He's sharp enough to spot real talent when he sees it."

After a few choice words about "the boy's" mentality, Jiggs returned to her studio, followed by their combined laughter. Alone with her drawings, she permitted a small chuckle to escape. She must have looked like a full-fledged, card-carrying idiot, chasing Ruth down the hall. She smothered her laughter with her hand as she recalled the way Ruth had hurried away as though the devil himself were at her heels.

She settled down to her work with a contented sigh. Never had she laughed as much as she had in the few short weeks that she had known Matt. He was always there to share in the warmth which surrounded her in his house, but he had never once pressed her for a more intimate relationship. He was giving her a chance to adjust at her own pace. Jiggs had never met anyone like him. The attraction she felt for him would have made it simple for him to seduce her, but by waiting he was showing her that he valued their friendship as much as she did. This was not the casual, when-it's-convenient friendship that Jiggs had found in the past. This was the old-fashioned, lasting kind. And she was coming to rely on his gentle understanding as well as the all-enveloping warmth that she felt in his presence. Matt seemed to be interested in every aspect of her life and she, in turn, devoured every bit of information about his life that came her way.

Saul occasionally joined them for dinner and it was through him that Jiggs learned of Matt's childhood. Matt's parents had been so caught up in the Texas political scene that they had had little time for their only child. Saul, at that time the caretaker of the exclusive boys' camp where Matt spent his summers, had unofficially adopted Matt as his own. The gruff recluse and the repressed little boy had become constant companions, and Saul had introduced Matt to the wonders of the magical kingdom he would later claim as his own.

When Matt and Saul spoke of their early days together, Jiggs could detect no resentment, no regret in Matt's memories of his parents, yet she knew that those years must have played a part in making him the man he was today.

As they sat together in front of the first fire of the season, she once again questioned him about his past, hoping to find a clue to his present character.

"When did you build this house, Matt?"

"Saul and I built it the summer and fall of the year I turned twenty—nineteen years ago." He joined her on the rug and leaned against the couch, pulling her with him. "I had gotten my B.S. that spring and Dad was pushing me to join him in the business, with an eye to a political career for me in the future. I refused point blank and he, in turn, refused to pay for the rest of my education." He stroked her hair unconsciously as he spoke. "He had a perfect right to spend his money as he saw fit, but there was a rather nasty argument, so I walked out.

"That was when I got the brilliant idea of hitching to California." He chuckled.

"Why California?"

"Why not?" Because it was there I guess. Anyway the trip out was a snap. I got lucky and hit the coast in only two days. The trip back was a different proposition entirely. I spent three days trying to get out of the damned desert. It finally got to the point that I was so desperate to hear the sound of another human voice, I started to throw rocks at passing cars, hoping that someone would stop, if only to punch me in the mouth."

"Matt, you didn't!" She laughed.

"Oh yes I did. It worked, too. I didn't get punched, but I did get a ride back to Texas. When I got back to Saul, I figured the time had come for me to make my own way in the world. So after a night of hard drinking, Saul and I pooled our resources, bought this land, and started clearing it."

"Saul got drunk, too?" she asked, unable to picture the tiny man inebriated.

"Did he ever! As he would put it, he was 'drunker than Cooter Brown.' He said a true friend shares everything—even tying one on."

"I like Saul, Matt." She smiled broadly. "He's the strangest man I've ever met, but he has a way of saying things that makes you really stop and think."

Matt hugged her briefly, as though she had pleased him, and they sat in companionable silence, watching the flickering fire. With her head on Matt's shoulder, Jiggs grew drowsy, hypnotized by the motion of the flames and the warmth of his body.

"Matt?" she murmured sleepily.

"Um," he answered, as though he too were in a semi-trance.

"Who's Cooter Brown?"

"What?" He shook himself awake and looked at her as if he had not heard her correctly.

"All my life I've heard of people being 'drunker than Cooter Brown,' but nobody has ever been able to tell me who he was. Apparently he was a Texas phenomenon, because people from out of state don't know what I'm talking abut. Do you know who he was?"

He rubbed his jaw thoughtfully. "No, now that you mention it, I can't say that I do. In fact . . ." his expression was a cross between suppressed laughter and accusation, ". . . you're the first person who's ever asked me the question."

"Oh, well," she sighed regretfully. "It's not really important. I just wondered. He must have been a powerful drinker to have everyone in the state of Texas talking about him."

"I suppose so," Matt agreed, settling back in their former comfortable position.

Several times in the next hour Jiggs attempted to make conversation, but Matt seemed preoccupied. She began to wonder if he had grown tired of waiting for their relationship to develop and had lost interest in her. If he's lost interest this quickly, she thought, it can't have meant much in the first place. She realized she was working herself into a fine state of annoyance, so she decided to go to bed before she made a fool of herself.

"Matt, I think I'll turn in now if you don't mind," she said, pulling away from him.

He looked at her thoughtfully, not seeing her, and, after a moment, said, "I'll bet Ian could find out."

"What? Matt, what are you talking about?" she asked, totally confused.

"Ian McKenzie knows every anthropologist in the state of Texas. One of them is bound to know who Cooter Brown was," he answered, enthusiastically.

"You idiot," she laughed, framing his face with her hands and kissing him soundly. "You're wonderful!"

"Are you just now discovering that?" he asked, bewildered but obviously pleased.

He smiled into her eyes and suddenly the air between them was electrified. With the gentlest of pressure he drew her closer. Jiggs didn't even try to resist. She knew she wanted, needed to be held by him. Slowly, never taking his eyes from her face, he lowered his head. Then when his lips were so close she could feel his warm breath, he stiffened and abruptly withdrew.

She could almost see him switch off the force that had drawn them irresistibly together. It seemed as though he had willfully destroyed the sensual empathy which had vibrated between them moments before.

"Matt?" she inquired hesitantly.

"You know, Jiggs," he said in a curiously edgy tone, "I've been thinking about that Pennsylvanian drawing. I think that instead of dividing the scene into part underwater and part shoreline you should do two separate drawings. It would give the reader a more accurate idea of the type of foliage that grew during that time period. And, of course, aesthetically it couldn't hurt to have more of the lushness that was typical of that climate."

Jiggs had to make a visible effort to keep her mouth from dropping open in astonishment. One minute they were on the verge of making love and the next they were discussing business. As much as she loved her work, this just didn't seem the time or place to iron out the details.

Why was he shutting her out like this? He had said more than once that he wanted their friendship to progress as quickly as possible, so why this abrupt about-face?

She tried to quiet her confused thoughts and concentrate on what he was saying, but as he talked on and on about the project in an oddly stilted voice she simply became more confused. He was going over procedures they had already discussed. The only possible reason he could have for bringing them up now was to establish a less intimate climate in the room.

Bewildered, she searched his face, hoping for a clue to his strange behavior, but he assiduously avoided her eyes, eventually rising to his feet and absentmindedly helping her to hers.

"You said something about being ready for bed, didn't you?" he asked. His casual manner seemed forced. "I don't want to keep you up. I know the work you're doing now is particularly delicate."

"Yes, I suppose it is," she agreed hesitantly. "Well, I—I'll see you tomorrow." Jiggs walked slowly to her room, confusion plaguing her thoughts. Surely a physical relationship was part of what they had each hoped for? Why had he pulled away at the last minute? It was almost a replay of their encounter in his penthouse. Only this time *he* had withdrawn. Was it some subtle form of torture he had devised to get even? If that was his plan, then it had worked beautifully. She was a mass of frustrated longing.

Frustration was to be her constant companion in the days to come. Every time she seemed to be getting close to Matt, he would back off abruptly. She had never chased a man in her life, but she definitely felt that Matt was running from her. His weird behavior was driving her crazy, the inner turmoil making it difficult for her to concentrate on her work, and sleep was impossible. She lay awake nights, torturing herself with memories of Matt's touch.

One day as she was filling in a particularly detailed section of an underwater scene, he appeared in the doorway of the studio he had furnished for her use. She looked up at him inquiringly.

"How would you like to play hooky?" he whispered conspiratorially.

Laying aside her brush, she regarded him suspiciously. "What did you have in mind?"

"Look outside, darlin'. It's a picnic kind of day." He pulled her to her feet and urged her to the window. "You see? That sunshine out there is just aching to shine on us. It would be a crime against nature to waste it. How about it, darlin'? It may be our last chance to swim this year."

His eagerness was irresistible. She was making very slow progress with her work, anyway. And a swim in that beautiful water sounded sinfully delicious. Matt was watching her with a pleading little boy look, waiting for her answer.

"Sure," she acquiesced. "I'd love it." The next moment she had to laugh as the little boy look disappeared and the efficient businessman took over.

"Great!" he said, pulling her out the door. "Go change into your swim suit and I'll ask Ruth to pack us a lunch."

After dragging her to her bedroom, and leaving her with a stern admonition not to dawdle, Matt continued on to the kitchen to confer with Ruth. Jiggs looked carefully at her slender arms in the bathroom mirror. "I don't think he's even aware of the way he pulls me around," she told her image in surprise. "There's probably some deep, psychological reason for this overwhelming need he has to see one of my arms longer than the other. Oh, well," she sighed, turning away to step out of her clothes. "It's not such a big thing. Everyone has a quirk or two—there's no need for me to mention it." She pulled on the bottom of her tiny black bikini, then turned again to address the sympathetic mirror with a thoughtful expression. "Of course, when I can scratch my knee without bending, I may say *something*."

Before she had finished fastening the top of her suit, she heard Matt pounding impatiently on the door and soon found herself trailing behind him, shrugging philosophically as he pulled her through the woods to the river.

They swam in the pool he had shown her that first day, diving from one of the monolithic boulders that appeared to be guarding the river. When Jiggs finally pleaded exhaustion they relaxed in the water, letting the current push them to the sandy bank where they had left their lunch. Ruth had packed enough for the proverbial army, but after their strenuous exercise it tasted absolutely ambrosial and they had no trouble doing full justice to it. Afterward they lay on a blanket, giving the sun a chance to do its thing on their drowsy bodies.

Jiggs awoke sometime later to the sound of gently splashing water and raised herself slightly to watch Matt emerge from the pool. His muscular, tanned body gleamed bronze in the sun. He was a mountain of a man. It didn't seem possible that he had been born of mere flesh and blood. His rough features and enormous strength looked as though they had been carved by the elements from virgin stone. This sort of natural beauty should have taken centuries to produce, not a paltry thirty-nine years. She watched, mesmerized, as a trickle of water blazed a trail through the curling hair of his chest, down his flat stomach, to be absorbed by his cut-off jeans which rode low on his hips. She caught her breath sharply as a piercing streak of desire hit her forcibly in the lower part of her body. Her vivid imagination spurred by pure lust had her following the water's course in her mind.

Scarlet flooded her face as she realized what she was doing and she jerked her eyes away from forbidden territory to find Matt watching her with a wide, pleased grin. He knew! The grinning idiot knew she was aching to touch him.

Jiggs responded to his knowledge in the only truly dignified way open to her. Rising to her feet, she pushed him—with dignity—into the river. The ensuing war was punctuated with cries for mercy— from Jiggs—and victorious laughter—from Matt. It ended with her ignominiously begging for a truce as he flung her to the rumpled blanket.

Straddling her body on his knees, he held her arms above her laughter-weakened form. "Now, me proud beauty, you'll pay for that bit of treachery," he said, leering evilly at her prostrate body.

"No, please, sir. Not that," she pleaded, breathless with laughter. "I'm saving myself for Burt Reynolds."

"I'm afraid Burt is doomed to disappointment," he murmured, lowering his head to tease her smiling lips.

The taste of him, the feel of him had filled every moment of her time—waking and sleeping—for what seemed like centuries and the first tentative touch of his lips triggered a wildly explosive response. She pulled her hands free to clasp his head, fearing he would once again withdraw, and hungrily searched the warm moistness of his mouth with her eager tongue.

She felt him gasp with surprise at her response, then he groaned as if in agony and rolled sideways, drawing her body to his in an exquisitely intimate, thoroughly possessive embrace.

"God, sweet! I've been going crazy these last few days." His laugh was rough and self-mocking. "If you had known the thoughts that have been running through my mind while I watched you paint, and watched you eat, and watched you curling up beside me like a trusting little kitten—you would have run in terror."

"You want to make a bet on that?" she whispered, sucking delicately on his earlobe. "Your acting ability—or my stupidity—is frightening, Matt. I thought you had changed your mind about wanting me."

He laughed shortly, pulling her closer in a bone-crushing bear hug. "You've got to be kidding. I thought I was being very obvious. Saul certainly noticed. Every time I see him lately he starts laughing, the wicked old goat."

"Well, why didn't you say something?" she said, punching him in the shoulder, then kissing the same spot as tears began to form in her green eyes. All that frustrated longing could have been avoided if she had only known.

He gently tilted her face, forcing her to expose the depth of her hunger. "Was it bad, baby?" he whispered, stroking the side of her face with his rough giant's hand, wiping away the tears with a calloused thumb.

"Oh, Matt," she sighed, digging her fingers urgently into his shoulders. "It's been hell."

He captured the sound of her pain with greedy lips, bringing a moan of pleasure from deep within her. Lifting his lips from hers, he sought the sun-warmed skin of her throat. A quivering tension was building inside her. By the time his thirsty mouth reached the rounded tops of her breasts, she was breathing in frantic gasps.

His trembling hands sought the clasp of her bikini in urgent, fumbling movements. "Sweetheart," he moaned, "I thought I could do this kind of thing blindfolded, but I think you're going to have to help me." He kissed the top of one full breast, his mouth seeking the treasure that was just out of reach. "And hurry, please, Jiggs, or I may rip the damn thing off." His intense words were muffled against her softness.

She reached behind her back to help with the clasp, exultant at the depth of his desire for her. Together they managed to undo the stubborn fastening and he impatiently pulled the flimsy covering from her eager, tumescent breasts.

With a sharply indrawn breath, he closed his eyes and gently touched first one, then the other taut, erect nipple. He seemed to be concentrating all his senses in the tips of his fingers, reveling in the feel of her obvious desire. The earthy, pagan pleasure visible in his strong face was the most erotic thing she had ever seen. She arched to his touch as a cat arches to the touch of its owner.

No longer able to sustain the slow, gentle movement, Matt clutched her roughly to his body. The feel of his hair-roughened chest and thighs against her softness was an exquisitely tactile delight and she clung violently, arching her hips convulsively, entwining her legs with his as though she would pull him into her body.

The frenzy of their movements brought a sheen

of perspiration to their writhing bodies. Matt clasped her buttocks with his large hands and began to blaze a fiery path down her body, trying frantically to quench an unquenchable thirst. He drank deeply from her heaving breasts, bringing moans of pleasure from her throat that increased the hunger of his searching mouth. He explored her ribs and the sensitive area of her navel, then slipped lower to the soft inner part of her thighs. Jiggs caught her breath in a tremulous gasp as he moved his head and suddenly, through the soft fabric of her bikini, she could feel his heated breath on that most vulnerable place, merging with the heat he had already kindled, the flame spreading like wildfire throughout her body.

Sounds began to penetrate her fevered mind. Strange whimpering sounds. And, from somewhere on a different level, she realized that Jiggs the strong, Jiggs the independent was whimpering in sheer, unadulterated pleasure. She was astounded that anyone could provoke such an unrestrained response from her. The incredible feeling of being immersed in sensation was too great to contain. She needed to show her joy in action. She wanted to share her pleasure, give measure for measure.

Jiggs slowly urged Matt's head up and, under his glazed, watchful eyes, began a reciprocal exploration of his body. The feel of the short, curling hair on his chest against her face was glorious. She tasted the damp saltiness of his skin, inhaled the scent of his masculinity. Her tongue on his hard, male nipples sent shudders of pleasure rippling through his body, an aphrodisiacal tremor to her seeking hands. His fingers were threaded through her disheveled auburn hair, not guiding, but a gentle affirmation of his pleasure in her wandering tongue. As she reached the top of his low-riding cut-offs, she felt him take a sharp, rasping breath.

"God, yes, sweetheart. Touch me," he groaned, his voice hoarse and urgent.

She moved her hand from his rock hard buttock slowly across his firm hip, caressing her way to his throbbing shaft of desire, then exhaled a soft, moaning breath as she found his pulsating strength.

The effect of her touch on Matt was explosive. He moved with swift urgency and suddenly she was beneath him feeling the hard, wonderful length of his body against the receptive softness of hers. His frantic mouth devoured her lips, his tongue plunging deep into the seductive depths of her mouth, then his lips moved to her vulnerable neck in search of more sweet sustenance.

In the dim reality of her mind, faint, intrusive noises—voices in the distance—began to penetrate. She lifted her leaden eyelids to look at Matt. "Matt?" she whispered hoarsely.

He raised his head to look at her lips as she spoke. His eyes had a wild, fiery gleam like a man possessed. "Yes, sweet."

That ragged voice couldn't belong to Matt. The wonder of his being so consumed by desire and the burning intensity of his stare put her intended question back where it belonged—in the realm of the real world that had no part of their tactile fantasia. A slight pressure brought his mouth back to her hungry lips where it belonged.

But the real world would not stay out for long. As Matt slid her legs apart to mold her more completely to him, the voices intruded again, this time louder and more difficult to ignore. He raised his head to look questioningly into her sensation-drugged eyes. "I don't think we're alone, darlin'," he whispered.

"Oh?" she replied lethargically. His lower lip suddenly seemed the most fascinating thing she had ever seen. She lifted her hand lazily from its resting place on his neck to trace the shape of it with one trembling finger. "You're a very dangerous man, Matt."

He gave a short, oddly tremulous laugh. "Where you're concerned, sweet witch, I'm a great, hulking bowl of jello."

Her hands moved to his broad shoulders, feeling his strength, denying his statement. She raised her head from the blanket to kiss the warm, tanned flesh. "Did you say something about our not being alone?" she asked with complete indifference, moving her hands down his back to his firm buttocks, exploring the rounded flesh thoroughly.

"I can't remember," he whispered huskily.

She arched her body against his in pleasure as his lips found the sensitive spot at the base of her neck and his hand stroked her thigh and hip, sending an erotic message to her impassioned body.

Turning on his side, he slid his hand inside her bikini and, with gentle tugs, was beginning to ease it off when a loud squeal of laughter disrupted their sensuous idyll. He sighed deeply and stroked her cheek with his calloused hand. "I'm afraid we can't ignore them any longer, darlin'." His wistful tone was comical and, at the same time, strangely moving.

He rolled onto his back abruptly, his body hitting the blanket with a disgusted thud. He lifted his eyes to the blue, cloudless sky and muttered in frustration, "Why me?"

Jiggs giggled helplessly at his exaggerated sigh, scrambling to find her bikini top and refasten it before they were face to face with the noisy group which seemed to be getting rapidly closer. The hook was hopelessly tangled and she broke into fresh laughter as she thought of how much trouble they'd had unfastening it.

"Matt," she cried, beginning to panic. "It won't hook."

He pushed her hands aside to try his luck with the recalcitrant hook. "Good Lord, darlin'. What did you do to it? It's twisted all around." He fumbled impatiently, jerking her backwards in his fight to the death. "What in the hell happened to buttons?"

"Matt!" she squealed as she twisted to look over her shoulder, trying to see what he was doing. "I refuse to go home wearing your shirt!"

"Stop wiggling or I'll never get it done," he demanded. "And if I can't get it fastened, you'll either wear the blanket or leaves because, if you'll remember, I didn't wear a shirt."

Jiggs heard a muffled sound from behind her and, ignoring his order, turned to look over her shoulder. "Matthew Brady, you're laughing!"

"I can't help it, darlin'. I was imagining Saul and Ruth's faces if you returned to the house wearing leaves." His laughter was no longer muffled. It rang across the river in a deep, rich peal.

After a few seconds of indignant silence, the mellow sound of his laughter wove a spell of pleasure around her and she joined him, leaning on his bare shoulder when he had finally triumphed over the demon hook. When they heard another shout from just around the bend they began to pack away the remains of the picnic. As they folded the blanket, they saw a fully-loaded canoe come around the bend.

"Canoes," Matt said, his tone disgusted. "As much as I love canoeing, I don't think I'll ever be

able to see another one without flinching." He
stood, hands on hips, watching the boat come
nearer. "Look at those idiots throwing beer cans
into the river," he said as though it were the last
straw. "They can't be experienced canoeists."

As Jiggs watched Matt, a devilish gleam appeared
in his eyes.

"Matt! What are you planning?" she asked suspiciously. His mischievous grin boded no good for
the unsuspecting intruders.

"Who, me?" The halo surrounding his angeli-
cally innocent face was slightly crooked.

"Matt," she repeated sternly.

"I was just thinking, darlin'. There's a place
about two hundred yards downriver from here,
right around the next bend, where the rocks sometimes give inexperienced canoeists a rough time."

She looked at him in alarm.

"Oh, nothing serious," he reassured her. "Just
a little, bitty chunk of white water. They'll only get
wet."

He reached for her and swung her surprised
form around in a joyously wide circle. "Let's go
watch them tip over, darlin'. I deserve that much
for the frustration they've caused. They should
have known I was loving my Jiggs on this part of
the river. Please, darlin,' " he coaxed, his little boy
look firmly in place. "Besides, we can pull them
out if they're too drunk to swim."

The belated addition of righteousness helped to
sway her and they ran like children, with clasped
hands, to the spot downriver. By the time they
arrived the first canoe had already floundered on
the small rapids and they rushed to help its pas-
sengers rescue their possessions.

As she worked, Jiggs recalled Matt's words. "My
Jiggs," he had said. Why didn't the implied pos-

sessiveness of those words bother her? Why did she melt a little inside when she remembered? She didn't want to be anyone's possession and the fact that his words didn't bother her, bothered her.

After Matt, having had his revenge, sent the dampened party on its way, the two of them walked back to pick up their things.

On the way home, Matt whistled cheerfully, pausing at frequent intervals to kiss Jiggs's slightly swollen lips. As much as she enjoyed being kissed by him, this delightful occupation couldn't stop the doubts from reverberating inside her brain. She knew he was expecting to take up where they had left off as soon as they were alone. And it was what she wanted also, wasn't it? All week she had been aching to be in Matt's arms, in Matt's bed. Why did her stupid brain have to get in her way now?

As she showered and changed, the doubts kept returning. He hadn't shown any signs of wanting anything more from her than a friendly affair, so why did she hesitate? His words by the river had meant nothing. If they made love it would only deepen their friendship. She could handle that.

"Well, I can," she belligerently told the doubtful face in her mirror. "So you can keep your opinion to yourself!"

All through dinner she felt Matt watching her— and Saul watching Matt watch her. She could see the questioning concern in Matt's eyes and made a determined effort to join in the conversation, but it was no use. The doubts that were swirling around in her head would not let her relax.

After what seemed like hours, Saul stood and bade them goodnight, his faded blue eyes twinkling with hidden merriment. He resembled an old elf enjoying the antics of a couple of frail human creatures.

Left alone with Matt, Jiggs decided finally and for all that she would not hesitate when he took her in his arms. It was what she wanted, she told herself, and she'd be damned if she would let her stubborn brain spoil her first night with him. A loving friendship was what she wanted and that was what he was offering her. She felt comfortable with Matt. She laughed with Matt. She lusted after Matt.

The miracle of his freely given friendship was unmatched by anything else in her·life. A total acceptance of her as she really was. He asked nothing from her except that she allow the friendship to grow and develop in other ways. He had expressed no desire to tie her down or absorb her personality. What they shared was so new and so precious she found herself wanting to protect it from any harmful influence. Even if that harmful influence was herself. It was the most wonderfully exciting thing that had ever happened to her and she wasn't going to let a little matter of semantics— those words "*my* Jiggs"—ruin it.

Having made up her mind, she waited impatiently for Matt to make his move. She glanced at him from the corner of her eye as he sat beside her on the couch. He seemed preoccupied as he watched the fire.

Maybe she should make a move. Her affair with Roger had been brief and uninspiring, teaching her none of the man-woman games people supposedly played, but surely she had enough feminine intuition, however atrophied, to carry off a simple seduction. Women throughout the centuries had been beguiling men with provocative looks and seductive poses. But Jiggs had the horrible suspicion that if she tried these artful measures, she wouldn't look seductive, she would look sick!

Oh, help! she silently pleaded. What in the world did she do now? Should she grab him and start kissing? No, definitely too crude. Maybe a subtle hand on his thigh? Oh, yes, touching his thigh would be nice, but was it the right move? Wasn't there some kind of signal that a woman gave a man when she was ready?

Lord, why hadn't she ever read any of those books all her friends had read? She bet none of them had a problem making a pass at a man.

"Jiggs, darlin', are you all right?"

She jumped guiltily at the sound of his voice. He was watching her closely, a strangely wistful smile playing about his firm lips.

"Yes, of course," she hastily assured him, trying to hide her chaotic thoughts. "Why do you ask?"

"The most intriguing expressions have been flitting across your face," he explained. "If I didn't know for a fact you didn't touch your dinner, I'd swear you had indigestion."

He pulled her into his arms and she snuggled closer. Returning his gaze to the flickering flames, he asked, "What's bothering you, Jiggs?"

"Nothing, really, Matt," she prevaricated. "I guess I just wanted you to hold me."

"Is that why you didn't eat any dinner?" He turned his head to look into her eyes. "It couldn't be because you were having second thoughts about this afternoon, could it?"

"No, of course—"

"Jiggs," he reprimanded. "The truth."

"Well, maybe a few tiny second thoughts," she admitted. "But they went away, honest."

"Tell me about it."

She looked thoughtfully into the fire, hesitant to discuss the subject since she had already decided to ignore her doubts. However, knowing Matt, he wouldn't rest until she had told him.

"It's not any one definite thing, Matt. I think part of it has to do with our friendship. I don't want you to think I'm saying 'poor, poor pitiful me,' but, as an adult, I've never had a real friend—not until I met you. And I value that friendship, Matt. *It's the most precious thing I've found in my life.* I don't want to jeopardize it. What would happen if we had an affair and then one of us wanted to call it off? Wouldn't that be the end of our friendship?" She looked him in the eyes and said candidly, "You're the most physically exciting man I've ever met, Matt. And I want you desperately, but from what I've heard desire doesn't always last very long. Should we take a chance on ruining a lasting friendship for the sake of a brief affair?" she asked earnestly.

For a while he simply stared into her face, then he sighed deeply. "So we have to choose between the two?" he asked. "I don't think you know either of us too well, darlin'. Personally, I think it would take more than a dead affair to ruin our friendship. There's something between us, Jiggs. I knew it the minute you opened your eyes that first morning. Something that won't go away no matter what happens." He sighed again, sounding tired for the first time since she had known him. "But that's not the real problem, is it, Jiggs? That's not the reason you were having second thoughts." His eyes were fixed intently on hers, demanding the truth.

"I said it was only part of the reason," she defended. "The rest is really too nebulous for me to put into words. It's just a vague feeling I had today on the riverbank. I felt as though things were going beyond my control. You know how I feel about sloppily emotional relationships. All my life, beginning with my own mother and father, I've seen what a man can do to a woman emotionally, if he chooses. It's not pleasant to watch, believe me." She shuddered in reminiscent horror. "A man can degrade and destroy a woman more quickly, through her emotions, than anything else on earth. I want no part of that sort of thing."

"So your parents had a bad marriage," he said scornfully. "Darlin', my parents forgot they even had a son until they wanted something from me, but I stopped letting that hurt me a long time ago. I can understand how your parents could have affected your view of life. But, Jiggs, you can't let that scare you into retreating from life. Someday you'll find something that's worth risking a little of that sloppy emotion on."

He stood abruptly and helped her to her feet, making no move to touch her, his features closed, almost cold. "But not tonight, darlin'. When you feel like making love to me is worth a little risk, you let me know."

As she undressed in her darkened room, Jiggs saw his face again in her mind. She had never seen Matt so forbidding. Was he angry at her reluctance? If she lost his friendship she didn't know what she would do. Maybe she should go to him, tell him that she was wrong, ask him to make love to her.

Her hand was on the doorknob before she came to her senses. She couldn't go to him like this, begging for his friendship. Matt wouldn't want her on those terms. She had to work things out in her own way. If he got tired of waiting, then the relationship wasn't as strong as it should be.

She walked to the window and stared into the moonlit night. She had a crushing feeling that it was going to be a very long night.

Suddenly Matt appeared on the deck, the moonlight glancing off his roughly chiseled features. She watched in silence as he leaned against the railing. He seemed deep in thought and—she drew in a harsh, pained breath—so terribly, terribly alone.

Seven

Jiggs sat staring at the preliminary sketch with disgust. It was simply awful. It looked stiff and amateurish. She ripped the offending sketch from her pad, crumpling it with suppressed violence. Nothing was going right and it was all Matt's fault. He had been away on business for three miserably long days.

At least he *said* it was business. He's probably visiting that little old brow-soother Barbie, she thought maliciously. He's probably playing doll house with her right now.

"What on earth is wrong with me?" she asked, revolted by her unreasonable bitchiness. She stood and walked to the window, remembering the way Matt had acted before he left. The coldness she had seen in his face on that disastrous night had been missing the next day. But so had the affectionate warmth she had come to count on. He had been polite, and interested in her welfare, the perfect host in fact. And all the while he had been holding himself from her. He had erected barriers that Jiggs couldn't penetrate. They had no longer laughed together. Finally in desperation, she had sought the company of Saul and even the stone-faced Ruth, rather than spend agonizing evenings with a stranger with Matt's face.

She had thought nothing could be worse than her deteriorating relationship with Matt. She was wrong. Being without him was worse, much worse. No matter how hard Saul and Ruth worked at trying to cheer her, the house seemed empty and curiously dead without Matt's vitality. Just knowing he was in the house, even if she weren't with him, made all the difference in the world. Saul was right. Matt was a part of the house—he was its heart. And without him the house was no longer alive.

She shook away the morbid thoughts and returned to her work. Not that she expected to accomplish anything, for her work had suffered dreadfully in Matt's absence. She couldn't seem to concentrate on what she was doing. She ripped page after ruined page from her drawing pad, finally laying her pencil aside in exasperation. It was useless to continue. She might as well take up needlepoint until Matt returned. She was so preoccupied with her aching feelings of loss of Matt that the notion she was coming to depend on him too much could only nibble at the edge of her mind.

"Do you want me to bring your dinner in here again, Jiggs?"

She looked up to see Ruth standing in the doorway and smiled ruefully. "I don't think I want anything tonight. Thank you, anyway, Ruth." Her appetite had been dwindling to the point of non-existence.

"Girl, you're going to be nothing but skin and

bones when Matt gets back if you keep this up," Ruth scolded. "You only picked at your lunch and toast is no kind of breakfast at all." Her tone was rich with disgust.

"I know, Ruth, and I'm sorry. I just don't seem to have much appetite," she apologized.

"Be that as it may, a body's got to have nourishment," she said pragmatically. "Now how about a nice bowl of soup?"

"Soup would be fine, Ruth," she acquiesced, knowing the woman's bland face hid a stubborn determination that was difficult to fight. "And I'll have it in here, please." The other rooms in the house were too evocative of Matt's absence.

As she watched Ruth leave, she wondered again what emotions lurked behind her expressionless face. Jiggs knew her lack of expression did not indicate a lack of intelligence or a lack of sensitivity, for she had come to know Ruth well and found she had a sharp mind. And although she could see no evidence of emotion in her face, Jiggs could feel warmth emanating from the older woman. She wondered what kind of childhood Ruth had had to cause that curious stone-featured facade. She would have to ask Matt when he returned.

Matt. It hadn't taken long for her thoughts to return to him. If only she had been able to hide her doubts from him, all this turmoil could have been avoided. But was that fair? Surely a good relationship deserved honesty? Yet she had been honest with him and what had it gotten her? He had forced the truth from her and then used that same truth against her. He was the one who wasn't being fair. He should have tried to understand. And how long was he supposed to go on understanding? she asked herself ruefully. At the rate she was going he could reach the age of eighty still asking, "Now, Jiggs?" She giggled at the thought of Matt, an old man with a cane, chasing her around a rocking chair.

For Pete's sake, give it up, Jiggs, she told herself. Don't think about it any more tonight. Excellent advice, but its effects barely lasted through dinner, dissipating entirely as she showered before going to bed.

The warm water caressing her exhausted body brought back memories of a rougher, more substantial caress. As she lathered her body, the sensations she had felt while in his arms, lying beneath his hard, male body, welled up with such strength that she cried out in anguish at her loss. After turning the cold water on full force, in a vain attempt to banish her erotic thoughts, she dried herself vigorously, each movement a chastisement for her errant body. She chose her nightgown carefully, avoiding the sensual silks, opting instead for a plain cotton shift. The warmth of her overheated body had not dissipated under the cold water and she paced the floor before flinging herself on the bed in disgust.

Twenty minutes later she knew she would not sleep tonight. She switched on the bedside lamp and picked up the book from the nightstand. Although she normally relished Goethe's every word, she was very much afraid this attempt at diversion would end like the others. She couldn't pull her thoughts away from Matt long enough to concentrate. Tonight she could see herself as Mephistopheles—a living spirit of negation. She had always considered herself to be optimistic in the extreme, but was she really? Wasn't she expecting the worst in her relationship with Matt? People who look for the worst, she told herself, always find it. Do I have so little faith in myself that I run from a situation because it could possibly be beyond my ken? So what if it turns out badly? Then I'll learn from it and next time I'll do better.

"I refuse to be Mephistopheles," she said aloud, slamming the book down on the nightstand. Scrambling from the bed, she grabbed her lightweight robe and stalked down the hall to the kitchen. She had never tasted warm milk, but if ever there was a time to try the repulsive sounding stuff, it was now. Anything was better than lying there, driving herself insane with thoughts of Matt.

She searched the cabinets for a small saucepan, poured in a cup of milk, then stood watching it, waiting for it to heat.

"How warm is it supposed to be, I wonder?" she mused aloud. "Why do I always read the wrong books? Betty Crocker or Julia Child would have been able to tell me how to heat milk," she muttered darkly. Since meeting Matt she had felt more inadequate about more things than she ever had before in her life.

I can't cook. I can't make up my mind. I can't even make a decent pass at a man, she thought in disgust. But I've got lots of good qualities, she mentally defended. I'm a good artist. No . . . I'm a damned good artist. I'm an adequate photographer. I'm a friend in need. I don't make noise when I eat jello. I look presentable—when I make the effort. And . . . and I'm cosmopolitan. I know enough Italian to sing along with Rossini, enough German to sing along with Lehar, enough French to order the right soup, and enough Spanish to get me out of El Paso.

"What more could I ask of myself?" she said aloud, then screeched in panic as milk boiled over the sides of the saucepan, pouring onto the stove.

"Damn, damn, *damn*!" She turned off the burner and grabbed a dish towel, wiping furiously at the revolting mess. "I can't even heat a simple cup of milk," she wailed, as though answering her earlier question.

Defeated, she laid aside the sopping wet towel and sat looking into space, silent tears streaming down her troubled face.

Look at me, she thought. This is the woman who didn't want to live life on a seesaw? No mental turmoil. No sloppy emotions. Ha! This is just about as sloppy as you can get. No matter what happens with Matt, things couldn't possibly be worse! I've got all the turmoil and none of the pleasure. It's not fair!

As she cleaned the stove she prayed for Matt's swift return. She plotted ways to show him she could handle an affair, but finally decided simply to tell him in plain English that she wanted him.

She walked into the hall, turning out the kitchen light as she left, then stopped for a moment, allowing her eyes to adjust to the darkness. As the furniture in the hall became distinguishable, something else became clear. Matt was standing in the hall not two feet away from her.

He stood, not speaking, looking so tired, she ached for him. His shirt was open at the neck and he had thrown his jacket over one strong shoulder. The need to move, to touch him was agonizing, but his silence held her still—until she looked at his tired face. A lock of brown hair had fallen forward on his forehead, lying neglected as though he were too weary to push it back. Slowly she extended her hand, gently smoothing the thick hair into place.

Her movement seemed to work as a catalyst, for with a deep groan, Matt pulled her into his arms and held her tightly as though he were afraid she would disappear. She cradled his head with her hands, stroking his face softly, murmuring words of comfort to soothe away his hurt.

"Oh God, baby," he moaned. "I need you." He didn't loosen his tight hold and made no move to kiss or caress her. He simply held her, trying to meld her body with his.

"I know, darling," she murmured. "I know. It'll be all right, you'll see. I'll make it all right for you." She whispered the words as though she were comforting an injured child, stroking his hair and neck, trying to make the hurt all better.

He laughed. A short, self-mocking sound in the darkness. "Jiggs, you idiot," he whispered, caressing her face with his own. "I'm not a child. I'm a man and my hurt won't go away with a band-aid or even a kiss—although a kiss might help."

"I know that, Matt," she answered solemnly. "I know how you hurt because I hurt in the same way."

He pulled away a fraction of an inch and looked into her eyes. "Sweetheart, I kept telling myself I would give you all the time you needed to make up your mind. That I wouldn't rush you." He closed his eyes and sighed deeply. "But I don't want to wait any longer. I'm not saying I won't, but I sure as hell don't want to. I need you to-night, Jiggs."

Cradling his face with her hands, she smoothed the troubled lines from his brow with gentle hands and softly whispered a will-o'-the-wisp kiss across his well-shaped lips. "Yes, please, Matt," she murmured. The words were finally out and a mixture of relief and nervous anticipation spread tremors throughout her body.

For a long moment Matt simply looked at her, feeling the trembling of her slender body. "You're sure? Jiggs, please be certain this is what you want." He brushed his lips across the top of her head. "I hope it is, sweetheart, because I don't think I can stop this time."

The look on his face was one Jiggs had never seen before, in fact she was quite sure it was an expression very few people had ever seen. Matt—as strong and self-confident as any man she had ever known—looked vulnerable. She had been so busy protecting her own vulnerability she had never considered the possibility that he too could be susceptible to hurt. That look of uncertainty stilled the trembling of her body and when he lifted her into his arms she sighed in pure joy, all doubt, all fear wiped away. She knew in that moment that whatever happened in the future, being in Matt's arms was indisputably, unequivocally right.

He carried her with swift, sure strides up to his bedroom and placed her on the outrageously large bed. He hesitated beside the bed as though unsure of his next move.

"Damn it, Jiggs. What kind of witch are you?" he muttered, raking his fingers through his thick hair. "I feel as nervous as a kid on his first parking date. What in the hell do I do now?"

A loving smile playing about her lips, she rose from the bed and drew a caressing hand across the hard muscles of his chest. "I'll bet if you really put your mind to it," she murmured in vampish tones, "it'll all come back to you."

"Imp!" He chuckled, grabbing her and pulling her to him abruptly, forcing the air from her lungs as her body made contact with his. "What am I going to do with you, you sweet idiot?"

"You mean you still don't remember?" she asked in disappointment.

She moved away and looked at him, intending to tease, but suddenly the air was fraught with electricity. The moonlight was streaming through the open windows and as she looked at him it seemed to her that his body was the most beautiful, the most perfect thing she had ever seen. She wanted—needed—to see him standing there in the moonlight, naked.

It never occurred to her to ask his permission. Compelled by a force beyond her control, she raised her hands and began to unbutton his shirt. His sharply indrawn breath didn't penetrate her intense concentration. Although she felt a deep urgency to see him unclothed, her movements were deliberately slow. She wanted to prolong the exquisite anticipation, reap the full benefits of the moment.

She spread his unbuttoned shirt wide across his chest, delighting in the feel of his warm skin and dark, curling hair. Kneading and stroking the muscles of his shoulders, she pushed his shirt aside. A gentle tug pulled the cotton shirt loose and it was discarded carelessly as she reveled in the sight of his bare upper torso. Caressing the now heaving chest with one hand, the other went willfully to his belt. She fumbled momentarily, bringing the other hand down to assist.

With a deep, shuddering groan, Matt took over from her groping hands and she moved back, the better to see him. In seconds he was free of the remaining garments. He moved toward her silently, then stopped as he took in the awe on her lovely face.

This was no Greek god she saw before her. This was all nature's rough beauty portrayed in vital, living flesh. No gentle lines and sleek form—he was pure, unadulterated male animal. Staring at his moon-glazed form, she knew she was seeing a basic truth, an honesty that had always escaped her.

"I was right," he whispered, wonder and something elusive in his tone, "you are a witch." He moved to stand before her, breaking the spell his hard, male beauty had cast upon her. He looked into her eyes as he touched her face softly and murmured, "You simply look at me and I feel things I've never felt before."

Jiggs turned her face into his large, calloused hand, kissing his palm. She felt a slight movement at her waist, on her shoulders, then her belted robe fell to the floor, lying at her feet like a discarded inhibition. He drew the cotton gown over her head, softly brushing her curves with his hand as he went, then stood, drinking in the subtly rounded softness of her slender shape. Her body shone, illuminated by an ethereal lunar spotlight. Later it would occur to her that she felt no embarrassment as he stared at her naked form. Matt seemed to be trying to memorize every part of her, his gaze lingering on her breasts, her thighs, the triangle of curling hair that spoke of her femininity.

When he picked her up and gently laid her on the bed, it seemed the most natural thing in the world. There was no hesitancy now for either of them. They were where they were destined to be—in each other's arms.

Resting on one elbow, he began to touch her face, exploring her high cheekbones, the softness of her eyelids, her sensitive lips. She lay motionless, eyes closed, as his hands moved lower to her body, absorbing his subtly erotic movements through every pore. It was a languid, drugging seduction of the senses. His hands were reaffirming the beauty his eyes had discovered before. As though still unconvinced, he followed the same path with his lips. The rate of his breathing increased, whispering a heated foretelling of each searching kiss.

As his hot breath and moist tongue gently teased her taut nipples, Jiggs felt a moan begin deep within her, shuddering its way to the surface, disrupting her motionless state.

Her quaking response was greeted by a short, triumphant sound from Matt and he cupped her now trembling breast, taking the erect tip deep within his mouth, then moved his hands to revel in the undulating softness of her hips.

Jiggs felt a burning ache in her loins—an agonizing urgency she had never experienced before. Her breathing accelerated to short, desperate gasps. "Matt," she moaned, pleading. "Please."

"Easy, sweet," he soothed, his voice raspy and strange. "Not yet. Just a little longer."

She groaned in frustration, grasping his thighs, his hard buttocks, trying to pull him closer. She gasped at the pleasure she felt at his uncontrollable shudder. To know her touch affected him so deeply was an unbelievable high.

"God, sweet!" he grated, as she grasped him boldly. His caressing hand moved to seek the heated moistness guarded by the curling triangle of hair. "So warm, so sweet. And it's all for me, isn't it, Jiggs?"

She trembled violently, making indistinguishable sounds in her throat as his fingers teased her to a frenzy. "Matt, damn it! Now!" she rasped harshly.

"Yes, by God! Now." And he raised above her, her eager hands guiding him to the source of her agony.

She moaned her pleasure as his hard shaft filled her. The feel of his manhood inside her was deliciously strange, yet unexplainably familiar. The slow, sensual strokes stoked the fiery tension inside her unbearably. He suddenly increased the pace of his lovemaking, carrying her away on a fantastic voyage with rhythmically orchestrated movements of exultation.

Her fingers dug sharply into his shoulders as she felt an intolerable pressure, a flaming hunger in her loins. She writhed in agony, her head thrashing wildly on the pillow. "Matt," she gasped, frightened by the intensity of the unfamiliar sensations. Then, "Matt!" in astonishment and wonder as she soared, leaving all earthly trappings behind. She rose to overwhelming heights before shuddering softly back to earth.

"Matt." This time the word was a sigh of loving gratitude—a gentle whisper of the pleasure still with her. She would have been terrified had she seen the adoration shining out of her eyes.

She wrapped her long legs around him, watching in fascination as he threw back his head, his rugged face contorted with the intensity of his pleasure. She rode out his storm with a warm feeling of *déjà vu*, cradling his gasping body as he reached his shuddering release.

They lay quietly for long, luxurious moments, bound together by exhaustion and the warm afterglow of love, then he propped his head in his hand, touching her swollen lips with one finger. "Well, darlin'," he whispered, smiling into her shining eyes, "didn't I tell you it was there inside you, waiting just for *me*." His voice was softly exultant—and a little smug.

"You're a conceited man, Matthew Brady." She laughed indulgently, kissing the tip of his finger, then stretched her body in a languorous, feline movement, bringing her arms to rest around his neck. "But I'll overlook it this time because you, my dear," she punctuated her words with tiny kisses on and around his mouth, ". . . are an amazing . . . example of . . . masculine . . . pulchritude." She laughed again, a delighted, exuberant sound of pure joy.

"Happy, sweet?"

"Happy! That doesn't come near describing it." She hugged him tightly, bursting with the incredible discovery she had made in his arms. "It's the most unbelievably intoxicating thing I've ever felt! I'm twenty-nine years old and I've just stumbled onto what it's all about." Genuine amazement was evident in her expressive features.

"Not stumbled, sweet," he whispered quietly, his face showing a momentary trace of guilt. "I'm afraid it was more a case of pushed."

Caught up in her own enthusiasm, Jiggs missed his barely audible words. "Why on earth didn't you tell me what it was like, Matt?"

He looked at her excited face for a moment, then laid his head on the pillow, cuddling her close with her head on his shoulder. "Would you have believed me? It's something you have to feel to believe!" He laughed softly. "And to tell you the truth, I wouldn't have been able to describe what just happened because it's something I've never felt before either."

His words brought a soft, warm glow to her body and she snuggled comfortably against him. They whispered and giggled like disobedient children far into the night, halting occasionally to speak with their bodies, and eventually dropping off into the deep, peaceful sleep of sated lovers.

Eight

Jiggs grunted disagreeably as bright sunshine inconsiderately struck her full in the face. With tightly closed eyes, she reached down to pull the cover over her head. Instead of a blanket, her fumbling fingers encountered a large, hairy object lying across her breasts.

"Matt," she sighed in sleepy satisfaction. Memories of the night before flooded her body, bringing a secret smile to her lips. She opened her eyes and looked at his sleeping form. Last night in the moonlight he had seemed unreal, unfamiliar to her unawakened senses. Today she knew every inch of him. She knew the scar on the back of one hard thigh, acquired while climbing—or rather falling from—a tree when he was ten. She knew the slight crook in one big toe—a gift from a disobliging cow at a dig in Africa. She was on speaking terms with the incredible strength in his arms, the ticklish spot on his back, and the errant curl at the nape of his neck. She knew his body better than she knew her own. And familiarity definitely did not breed contempt in this case. Her fingers itched to touch him again—to visit well-loved places—but the pleasure of watching him sleep held her back. She wanted to taste the full range of emotions in this loving friendship.

He had been so unbelievably gentle last night, so warmly affectionate. And then at times she had sensed a strange desperation in his loving, as though he needed to store up her warmth against hard times. But however he made love to her—gently or with a raging hunger—she reveled in it. And greedily she wanted more.

Matt stirred slightly, the movement causing the blanket to slip low on his hips. God! she thought, drawing in a small, sharp breath, his was the most erotic centerfold pose she had ever seen. The blanket was draped with almost purposeful discretion, showing his lean, dark hips and the flat plane of his stomach, but enticing the mind to imagine the rest.

Only I don't have to imagine, she thought, closing her eyes and smiling smugly. I have first-hand knowledge of how beautifully all his parts match.

"My, my," a drowsy, amused voice reached her ears. "You look like you've just discovered that Mrs. Reagan buys her clothes off the rack."

"Better," she murmured, opening her eyes to see his face smiling down at her. "Much, much better." She looked him over in mock surprise. "Haven't we met before? I seem to recall waking once before to find a man who looked just like you in the bed."

"And I remember waking, feeling more frustrated than I ever had in my life." He chuckled. "But of course, at the time I didn't know what was in store for me. I've learned that what I felt that night was mild compared to what I've felt since."

He shook her shoulder in gentle reproof. "You certainly believe in trial by fire."

He rolled onto his back, pulling her on top of him. "But for what you gave me last night, darlin', I would gladly suffer all that and more."

"My pleasure, I'm sure," she said demurely, earning a sharp, vaguely erotic slap on the derrière.

Suddenly she rolled off him and sat up. "Oh Lord, Matt!" She looked at him in horror. "What time is it?"

He glanced at the alarm clock on the nightstand. "It's ten. Why?" he asked, surprised at her abrupt actions.

"Ruth, Matt! Ruth!" She shook his shoulders to make him understand. "She brings my coffee every morning at seven. She must know by now that I didn't sleep in my room last night."

"I'm sure she does," he said matter-of-factly. "Because, you see, darlin'," he grinned irritatingly at her agitation, ". . . she brings *my* coffee every morning at six-thirty." He gestured to two cups sitting on the nightstand. Two cups!

"Oh, no," she moaned, sliding down in the bed and pulling the sheet over her head in misery.

He listened patiently to the unintelligible mumbles coming from beneath the sheet, then gently pulled it aside.

"Sweetheart, I can't understand a word you're saying. You'll have to take the sheet out of your mouth if you want to tell me about it." He gave her a stern look. "Now—slowly—tell me what's bothering you. I know you're not ashamed of sleeping with me because you didn't mind Saul knowing how we felt."

"Of course I'm not ashamed of it!" she repudiated indignantly. "But Ruth is different, Matt. She's—she's—American Gothic! I like her and I don't want her to think I'm a—a hussy."

Matt laughed in sheer delight. "But you are. A thoroughly brazen hussy," he said, hugging her to him. "Jiggs, you baby, haven't you seen the looks Ruth and Saul have been giving us ever since you arrived?"

"No," she said thoughtfully, trying to remember anything unusual in the way the older couple had looked at her, then finally admitted, "I guess I was thinking about . . . um . . . other things."

"Well, if you had been looking around, you would have seen that they both knew what was going on and what's more, my adorable blockhead, they probably think we were crazy to wait so long."

"Do you really think so?" she asked hopefully.

"Of course. Now stop worrying and kiss me, woman," he ordered, then as she stared at him in haughty inquiry, he added meekly, "Please."

"That's better." She looked at him in thoughtful consideration. "I suppose after all the strain you put on your decrepit body for me, you deserve a reward. Pucker up."

She squeaked in mock terror as he moved swiftly and moments later had pinned her laughing form beneath his giant frame. "Decrepit? Is that what you said, Jiggs?"

"I think you must have mistaken my words, darling," she said, gasping for breath beneath him. She felt his chuckle shaking her body and looked at him in bewilderment. "Were you this heavy last night?"

The chuckle grew into a laugh, rocking her violently. "Matt! For heaven's sake, stop laughing before I'm permanently disabled!"

"Am I heavy, sweet?" he asked considerately.

"Yes," she muttered with what felt like her last breath, squirming beneath him. "And you're not my brother either."

"Thank God," he breathed sincerely.

His voice sounded strange and Jiggs started to question the cause, but stopped at the look in his eyes. She caught her breath and, miraculously, his body no longer felt heavy. It felt exactly right.

"Matt," she murmured softly, "shouldn't we go have breakfast or something?"

"We'll have the 'something' now, sweet witch. Breakfast can wait." And it did.

As they sat down for breakfast at three o'clock that afternoon, they listened contentedly to Ruth scolding them for neglecting their food. She served them plates heaping with eggs, potatoes, and steak, then stood and watched as they fell on it voraciously.

"Well, it's about time. You, young lady, haven't eaten enough to keep body and soul together since Matt left." She looked at Jiggs as she scolded, her expressionless face giving the words a curiously mechanical sound. "And now you don't eat breakfast 'til it's nearly time for dinner. What's gotten into you, girl?"

It was definitely the wrong question to ask. Startled, Jiggs and Matt looked at each other, faces red with suppressed laughter, then, together, slowly they turned to face Ruth.

She looked at them for a moment with her usual non-expression, then an incredible sound split the silence.

When Ruth left the room, Jiggs looked at Matt, shock holding her face rigid. "Matt, was that—"

"I don't believe it," he said, shaking his head in bewilderment. "A smile would have been a shock. But, Jiggs . . ." he looked at her, his face comical with astonishment, ". . . that was an honest to God *guffaw!*"

It was some time before they could control their laughter enough to eat. Every time Jiggs thought of the look on Matt's face she broke up again.

When he left the table to consult with Saul, she sat quietly thinking how the world seemed to be smiling at them today. Ruth's incredible laugh was only a part of the magic. The house seemed to be laughing in delighted approval of their union.

In Matt Jiggs had someone with whom she could share all the incredible wonders, all the human comedy abounding in the world around them. This was truly the loving friendship she had sought. Never again would she have to suffer a deliciously funny incident in silence. Matt would never look at her in confusion and say, "What are you talking about?" He appreciated the subtleties and satire that occurred with astonishing regularity in day-to-day living.

Someone to laugh with. She now realized the importance of those words. She hadn't known what she was missing until she met Matt. There was a special communication between them. An invisible line that tied them mind to mind, soul to soul. When Matt saw or heard something that struck a chord within him, he simply glanced at her and she understood. Although their backgrounds were totally different, it was as though the basic ingredients of their separate personalities matched perfectly—a fact that seemed to amaze and delight Matt as much as it did her. He was constantly touching her. Not in a possessive, or even in a sensual way, but simply a gentle affirmation of her presence. His joy in their friendship kept her wrapped in a warm glow that made every moment with him different and special. Things that were nice before suddenly became poignant and wonderful in Matt's company. And things that were merely funny suddenly became hilarious.

And, at last, she understood what Saul had

been trying to say the day she arrived. There was nothing gaudy or flowery about Matt's friendship. It was basic and honest and real. The sort of thing that would stand when other more tenuous friendships fell. Saul had, in his own way, been warning her to value that honesty, but Jiggs needed no warning. She had seen enough artificial relationships to cherish the real thing when it came along. She would not take the risk of losing the special rapport that they shared.

She hugged herself with the thought of sharing with Matt. Last night she had discovered something wonderful in his arms and, like a child after its first taste of ice cream, ordinary fare would never again suffice. She was torn between the desire to hide away and relive each precious memory and the consuming need to make new ones.

This kind of affair—this loving friendship—was perfect. Her equation had worked after all. She would have all the highs, but none of the depressing lows of what was popularly known as love. She would be free of the ties and the helplessness that plagued those caught in the throes of that erratic emotion. A good solid friendship that would last a lifetime. And no worries about unfaithfulness or any of the other indignities constantly being perpetrated by lovers the world over. One is not unfaithful to a friend. The easy relationship eliminates the need for that type of devious behavior.

She leaned back in her chair with a contented sigh, totally satisfied with her life. She conveniently overlooked all the agony of the last few days as she thought smugly: No possessiveness. No jealousy. No emotional tangles that constantly need unraveling. Just warmth and laughter and companionship in their wonderfully uncomplicated friendship.

"What are you thinking about with such deep concentration?" He had entered her studio silently and was noisily nuzzling her neck as he spoke.

"Matt, stop," she laughed. "You sound like a pig, rooting around on my neck."

"Come on, darlin'," he said, giving her neck one last snorting kiss, then pulling her to her feet. "There's a beautiful day waiting for us." He grinned cockily. "At least, what's left of it is waiting for us."

"I hate to interject any vulgar practicality, but shouldn't we be working?" she asked, smiling at his enthusiasm.

"Now you're thinking like a mortal," he admonished. "If you want to fly on my cloud, you're going to have to make some radical changes."

"What model is your cloud?" she asked suspiciously.

"Well, actually it's a Jeep Wagoneer, but it'll have to do until I can check into the price of a used cumulus." He chuckled.

Oh Lord, here we go again, she thought, rolling her eyes as he pulled her through the front door and halted beside the large square vehicle. "Matt, darling, where are we going?" she asked with sweet patience, surreptitiously checking the length of her right arm against her left.

"It's fall, Jiggs," he said, gesturing around them. "And Palo Pinto County is all dressed up in her Sunday best. We're going to pay homage to a glorious season. Revel in the splendiferous beauty of nature."

"Does that mean we're going for a drive in the country?" she asked guilelessly.

"Philistine," he said, chuckling as she climbed into the high seat.

They drove through the country, stopping occasionally to enjoy a particularly beautiful setting.

They followed narrow side roads to their ends—usually at the front yards of tiny, white frame houses. Jiggs was seeing the world with new eyes. The riotous colors of autumn had never seemed so brilliant. The air was crisp and clean. She wasn't only seeing the world, she was tasting it—absorbing it into her body until she was a part of it.

They returned home for a very late dinner, hurrying guiltily at Ruth's muttered reproaches.

After dinner they strolled arm in arm to Saul's campfire by the river. The wizened old man watched them approach, his eyes twinkling in the firelight.

"You two look like it just rained after a long dry spell," he chuckled. " 'Bout time, too. I've seen dumb in my day, but you kids take the cake."

Matt hugged Jiggs tightly, whispering "I told you so" softly in her ear. She punched him sharply in the ribs and turned to Saul. "Are you from around here, Saul?" she asked, anxious to change the subject.

"Born and raised 'bout five miles from here," he confirmed proudly. "And my daddy 'fore me and his daddy 'fore him."

"You love it, don't you?" she asked softly.

He looked at her sternly. "I *know* it. My family's always been farmers and this land made 'em old 'fore their time. It's hard country. If the drought or flood don't get you, a tornado will. But look at it, girl." He looked like a miniature Merlin, casting spells in the firelight, as he motioned to the trees and the river, then whispered reverently, "Lord, it's beautiful."

Jiggs stood silently in the warm circle of Matt's arms, contentment filling her to the brim, as he and Saul quietly discussed the way the fish were biting.

In the days that followed, her contentment grew. At Matt's insistence, they postponed their work until they could get the strength to force their feet to touch ground. They spent long, lazy days exploring the woods and long, lazy nights exploring each other. They made love in the warm glow of the fire and on the soft, fallen leaves in the woods. They were on a whirling carousel that kept them dizzy with delight.

And always—day or night, laughing or loving—Matt watched her, a strange, waiting look in his eyes.

Two weeks passed unnoticed before Jiggs insisted they spend a part of each day working. She felt guilty about keeping Matt from his book and she also needed to express some of her overflowing joy in her painting. She threw herself into her work with an unequaled fervor, feeling that she had never painted so well. Fantastic, long-dead worlds sprang from her brush; exotic creatures took life under her flying pencil.

She giggled as she erased a knowing wink from the eye of an enormous prehistoric fish, then stretched her stiff back and want in search of Matt. She hadn't seen him in three hours and she missed him.

She met him in the hall on his way to find her. He pulled her into his arms and breathed a husky sigh in her ear. "I think I'm having withdrawal symptoms, sweet," he whispered softly. "I haven't kissed you in three hours."

"So long," she sympathized, playing with the wayward curl at the nape of his neck. "Are you sure your lips aren't atrophied?"

He drew his lips slowly across her cheek in a sensuous, tingling caress and paused before tracing the outline of her sensitive mouth with his tongue. Nipping gently at her lower lip, he teased her until she was giddy with desire, then began an erotic exploration of the inner sweetness in a deep, breathless kiss.

Jiggs leaned against him weakly as they walked to sit before the fire. "They're fine, Matt," she told him with lethargic complacency.

"Who's fine?" He pulled her into his lap and began to toy with the top button of her silk blouse.

"Your lips," she explained, leaning against his shoulder. "I just thought you'd like to know. They're fine. Not a sign of atrophy."

"Minx." He chuckled, undoing the button and moving to the next.

Jiggs looked into his beautiful, rough face and sighed. He was so perfect. At times she felt inadequate beside his perfection. But he didn't seem to mind her many imperfections. He loved the strawberry birthmark on her derrière and gloried in the riotous curls of her auburn hair when damp weather made it frizz.

"I was right and you were wrong," she told him smugly, remembering.

"About what?" He looked at her in exaggerated disbelief.

"About the loving friendship. You said I had it figured all wrong. But I was right and you were wrong. So admit it."

For a moment Jiggs saw a look of such deep sadness—almost pain—in his dark eyes, it alarmed her. "Matt, what is it?"

He closed his eyes tightly, leaning his head on the couch, then when he opened them again, it was gone. "Nothing, Jiggs. Just a case of incipient stupidity," he muttered obscurely, then at her questioning look, "It was nothing really, darlin', and as to your observation, I believe *I* was the one who said anything's possible, remember?"

"You only said that to make me feel better," she replied indignantly.

"No," he said with a crooked, self-mocking smile. "I really believed it—then."

As she began to question his ambiguity, he covered her mouth with his hand. "Jiggs, are we or are we not having an affair?"

She removed his hand and smiled lovingly. "We are."

"Then please be quiet so we can get on with it. You don't seem to be taking this seriously, darlin'. A successful affair takes practice, practice, and more practice. Understand?"

"Yes, sir," she said meekly, then sighed as they "got on with it."

Later that same night, Jiggs awoke to find the bed beside her empty. For a moment she felt an unreasonable panic take over—until she saw Matt standing by the window, looking out at the still, moonlit night. "Matt?" she murmured, still not fully awake.

He turned to see her sitting up in bed. "Go back to sleep, sweet," he said softly. "I'll be there in a minute."

His face held the same expression that it had the first time she had seen him in the moonlight. The night that—unaware of her observation—he had leaned against the rail, looking so desperately alone. Why should he feel a loneliness that deep? She thought she knew him so well. But was there something about him, something in his background, that he had hidden from her? Or was it something he needed that she was unable to supply? As his friend—his *best* friend, she corrected her thought—he should be able to talk to her about anything that was bothering him. Maybe she had been so busy thinking about how well he satisfied her needs, that she had not been sensitive to his. She had been so thrilled to find someone to share her laughter, but maybe Matt needed someone to share his tears.

She rose silently from the bed, drawing on her robe, and walked to stand beside him, laying a hand on his shoulder. "Matt," she said quietly. "I haven't been a very good friend, have I?"

He laid his cheek on her hand, rubbing it gently. "What makes you ask that, sweet?"

"I've been so wrapped up in my own pleasure that I completely missed the fact that something is bothering you." She turned his head slightly so that she could see his face. "Can't you tell me about it, Matt?"

"It's nothing, Jiggs," he denied, then as she was about to protest, "Honest. I was just thinking."

"About what?"

"Oh—about cabbages and kings and sealing wax—and the fact that a man can live a perfectly content life for years, then one day, something happens that turns everything around and makes those years seem wasted and empty." His voice was quiet and, strangely, a little lost.

"Are you regretting your past, Matt?"

"Not regretting." He put his arm around her and walked her to the bed. "Just an observation. And now, young lady, let's go back to bed and get some sleep or you'll have bags under those lovely eyes."

She paused before getting into bed. "Matt, do you need some time alone? Would you like me to sleep in my bed tonight?"

"*This* is your bed, sweetheart. So don't talk about leaving me alone." He hugged her to him tightly when they were both in the large bed. "This is where you belong, isn't it, Jiggs?" His voice sounded odd, as though he were painfully in need of reassurance.

She murmured soft, loving words in his ear and stroked his body until his doubts were forgotten and he took her with a ravenous hunger.

The next morning she watched him closely, but saw no signs of last night's strange mood. Everyone is entitled to a little moodiness now and then, she thought. Just wait until he sees me after one of my sinus headaches.

After breakfast she worked on a sketch of one of the rarer, more intricate trilobites. One particular detail kept giving her trouble, so she finally laid it aside and went in search of Matt, hoping he could clear up her confusion.

She stopped outside his study as she heard his voice.

"No, Barbie, of course not."

Barbie! Jiggs had completely forgotten about the beautiful redhead. Why was Matt talking to her? She stepped closer to hear what he was saying. Jiggs, she scolded herself, you're eavesdropping. No, I'm not, she defended, I'm simply waiting until he's through so that I can speak to him.

"Barbie, I told you before that I wasn't angry. I understand completely, sugar. There was nothing else you could do."

It was no use. No matter how much she rationalized it, it was eavesdropping. She walked slowly back to her studio, turning her head occasionally to glare at the open door of his study.

Barbie, she thought again, nonplussed. Who was Barbie anyway? And what did she mean to Matt? What had he said about her that night? He had called her a friend—"a brow soothing friend." And what else did she soothe? They had obviously had an affair, for he had asked Barbie to stay at the hotel with him. Was it a long-standing affair?

An off again—on again thing? Maybe Jiggs had met Matt during one of the off again times.

Damn him! He had no business carrying on with two women at the same time. It wasn't fair and it wasn't neat and it wasn't . . . kosher! How could he make love to Barbie when he belonged to—

Oh my God! She buried her face in her hands as she completed the thought. He belongs to me. Possessiveness. Jealousy. All the things she swore she would avoid. Things she now realized she had been feeling since she first met Matt.

I love him, she thought in horror. Sloppily, emotionally, possessively—I love him.

What in the hell am I going to do? She didn't want to be in love. Her mother had been in love and look what it had gotten her. A lifetime of degradation. And those silly women at work— crying in the ladies' room, unable to do their jobs. She was one of those silly women now and she hated the thought, hated Matt for making her feel this way. She had simply wanted a nice, friendly affair. Where did she go wrong? Why did it have to be love?

Lord, I'm so stupid, she thought in disgust. Any idiot would have seen what was happening. I couldn't keep my hands off him—or my mind. And every time I thought of him I could feel that silly, simple-minded grin on my face. Of course, I love Matt. Anyone could see that. Anyone except me.

Matt! How on earth was she going to face him? After all her fine talk about no emotional tangles she had to go and fall in love with him—and he would know! She could never hide what she was feeling from him. He seemed to be able to read her mind.

She stood and began to pace back and forth,

kicking the chair viciously as it got in her way. She couldn't let Matt find out! They had agreed to have an affair—a loving friendship. He would be embarrassed when he realized she had fallen in love with him. The thought of Matt pitying her made her shudder. They had always met as equals, but his pity would diminish her in his eyes—and her own. Pity was the only emotion she knew that was more destructive than love and a relationship that contained both elements could only humiliate the people involved.

She had to get away. She couldn't face Matt right now. She would go back to her apartment for a few days and think things through alone. Maybe in time she would think of a way without losing her self-respect to tell him why she must end their affair. It would mean giving up her job also, for she would never be able to work with Matt without touching him . . . loving him.

She hurried to their room for her purse, praying he wouldn't come out of his study before she got safely away. She had to leave a note for him and she hesitated briefly, trying to find the right words, but it was impossible. Nothing would explain adequately her running away. In the end, she decided to keep it simple and avoid fabrication. She wrote that she had decided to go away for a few days and would call him later to explain. It was woefully insufficient, but it was the best she could do in the circumstances.

She felt like a thief, creeping silently down the hall and out the front door, but she knew she would dissolve ignominiously in tears if Matt caught her. She stood in the shadows inside the garage and fumbled nervously for her keys.

"Going somewhere?"

Jiggs jumped and whirled in absolute terror at the sound of the voice behind her, then sighed in relief as she realized the voice and tiny form couldn't possibly belong to Matt.

"Oh, Saul," she said, "you scared me."

"You got a guilty conscience, girl?" The little man looked at her suspiciously.

"I'm not making off with the family silver, if that's what you mean. I just decided to get away for a few days."

"You tell Matt?"

She looked away from him, avoiding his eyes. "I left a note."

"A note?" He snorted in disbelief. "You coulda' hollered as you went out the door if you're in a hurry. He's right there in the house."

Jiggs closed her eyes, desperation to be on her way building unbearably, then looked at Saul with a sigh of resignation. "I just can't talk to Matt right now." Her eyes pleaded with him to understand. "I've got to get away for a while, Saul."

His keen eyes pierced her, searching her face. "I guess you do at that, girl. Go on, Jiggs. And be careful—it's comin' on to rain."

It would hurt to lose this man's friendship, too. Jiggs shuddered in sudden loneliness, then bent down to kiss his weathered cheek. "Thank you, Saul."

He stood in the yard and watched her back out of the drive. She gave the house one last, longing look, then headed east.

Nine

The rain that followed Jiggs all the way to Dallas was the perfect setting for her black mood. She turned her radio up to an ear-splitting volume, trying to drown her thoughts, but she only succeeded in making her head ache as well as her heart.

Even though the rain had slowed her down, she still beat the afternoon rush and by four o'clock she was pulling into the covered parking space in front of her apartment. The driving rain turned her blouse into a transparent second skin and she shivered uncontrollably as she reached her door and inserted the key.

She was home. Home. This empty apartment wasn't home. Home was warm and welcoming. Home was love and laughter. Home was Matt.

The tears streaming unheeded down her face mingled with the raindrops as she stood in the middle of the large, lonely room, looking for all the world like a lost child. And she felt lost. She felt as though she had been cast out of paradise. Somewhere east of Eden, she thought with a choking, sardonic laugh.

She moved slowly, wearily toward the bedroom, intending to change her clothes, then halted in her tracks as the ringing of the telephone broke the stillness.

Matt!

She couldn't talk to him. She moved in panic toward the bedroom, but the insistent ring drew her back. I've got nowhere else to run to, she thought. The terrible weariness had completely sapped her strength and the fight drained out of her, leaving her empty of emotion.

She walked to the phone, an unnatural calm showing in her face.

"Hello?"

"Jiggs! Is that you?"

It was Max. Relief buckled her knees and she sat down heavily in a high-backed armchair.

"Yes. It's me." There was a slight tremor in her voice and she ran a shaking hand over her damp face, trying to pull herself together.

"You sound strange. Are you all right?" His voice held concern.

"I'm fine, Max."

"You don't sound fine. You sound sick. And you haven't asked why I'm in town. I'm supposed to be in Europe, remember?"

"Oh, Max, I'm sorry. Of course, you are. I forgot." She tried to think. What should she say now? Obviously, words were expected from her, but which words? She was very much afraid anything she said would come out complete nonsense.

"Jiggs!" Now his voice held more than concern— it held a distinct uneasiness. "Stay right where you are!" he commanded anxiously. "I'll be right over."

"No, Max . . ." But the connection was broken. He was already on his way.

She stared at the phone in her hand for a moment, then replaced it lethargically. She felt she should move. Maybe change into dry clothes or brush her hair, but by the time she had definitely decided to do *something*, she heard Max's knock on the door.

"Jiggs! Jiggs, you're wet!" he exclaimed as she opened the door.

"I know," she said, looking down at her clothes which had begun to dry on her body. "I meant to change, Max, but—"

"I know, you forgot," he finished for her. "First we're going to get you into a hot tub, then—we talk."

He brushed aside her halfhearted protests, steering her to the bathroom. She leaned against the door and watched as he filled the tub, testing the water carefully and adding scented bathsalts.

"Now hop in and don't take too long or I'll come in and get you," he warned.

She removed her uncomfortably damp clothes, sighing in pleasure as she stepped into the steaming water. She relaxed for long moments, letting the warmth soak in and soothe away the cold tiredness. When she returned to the living room, she could face Max with a semblance of normalcy.

He rose to watch her closely as she crossed the room to stand before him. "Now, let's talk." His voice was uncompromising, warning her not to prevaricate. "What happened?"

She sat beside him on the loveseat and looked at his thin face. She felt she was truly seeing him for the first time. "You know, Max, I was wrong. I did have a friend. At least I could have had one if I had just opened my eyes." She touched his face, surprised at how much she liked this man. It seemed that loving Matt had pulled a dark veil from her eyes and her mind. She would never be able to hide from emotion again. The realization made her shiver in apprehension. She looked up to find Max watching her through narrowed, piercing eyes. "You really are a nice man, Max. I should have been a better friend to you."

Max sighed, a thin hissing sound. "I always knew it would happen, sugar. And now that it has, I don't know whether to be thankful for your sake or sorry for mine." His tone was wry and perhaps a shade cynical.

"What are you talking about?"

"Well, sugar, you've either joined one of those encounter groups or you're in love."

She looked at him in amazement. "My God, Max! Is it written in 'Marks-a-Lot' on my forehead? Am I really that obvious?"

"No, not obvious," he reassured her. "But I've spent quite a bit of time studying you, Jiggs. I take my role as scorekeeper for the human race very seriously, you know." He allowed a touch of his usual mocking humor to show. "And you, Toots, make one interesting subject. You always held yourself away from life, as though you were on a different plane from us lesser mortals." When she looked at him in alarm he added, "I don't mean snobbish, Jiggs. You didn't think you were better than us, just different. You were interested in everything and everyone around you, but you didn't participate. You were a spectator. And that's fine for football, but not in life."

She could see the truth in his words—now. And she could also see how much she had missed. No matter what he said, her attitude had been a form of snobbishness. She had felt unutterably smug at not being subject to the emotions that others felt. Now she simply felt sadness for the time she had wasted.

"I knew that if you ever found someone who could make you feel love, it would open the floodgates for all the other emotions."

"Was I so unfeeling, Max?" she asked, concerned. "I know I felt an unforgivable pride in what I considered my strength, but was that all? I guess it's pride again, but I hate to think of myself as an automaton."

He put a comforting arm around her shoulder. "You were a sucker for every hard luck story and you know it," he reassured her. "But there were times when you were, shall we say, unsympathetic to those who were slaves to their emotions. I didn't really blame you. They get on my nerves, too, but it worried me because you're so soft-hearted, you should have felt something for the poor slobs. Then I realized that you felt nothing for them because you had locked away the part of you that would have recognized love and passion."

"Whew!" she said, laughing ruefully. "I didn't realize I was in such bad shape."

"Your shape is great," he said, leering. "It's the emotional part of your mind that's screwed up."

"Thanks a lot," she muttered drily. "Since you were so concerned about me before, I guess it pleases you that I have unlocked all the doors and joined the human race."

"It's healthier, Jiggs. Even if it hurts like hell now." He paused, looking at the floor, then said quietly, "Do you want to tell me about it?"

His gentle understanding brought a sheen of tears to her green eyes. "I don't think I can right now, Max. But—" She hesitated momentarily, then plunged into unknown territory. "—If you'll hold the thought until your assignment is finished,

I—I think I would like to tell you. And maybe by then I'll be able to." She looked at him shyly, feeling incredibly vulnerable.

He accepted her gift, recognizing its true value. "Anytime, Jiggs. All you have to do is call."

She kissed his cheek softly, overwhelmingly relieved that he had understood her gesture of friendship. Suddenly she looked at him in surprise. "Max! What are you doing in Dallas? You're supposed to be in Europe!"

He chuckled, squeezing her shoulder affectionately. "You're a little slow, kid. But I'll overlook it this time because what you lack in mental ability, you make up for in physical splendor."

Overlooking his comment on her body as she usually did, she looked at him in concern. "Nothing went wrong with the assignment, did it?" She knew how much the series meant to Max. If it fell through now, it would be a terrible disappointment.

"Nothing that I can't handle," he said arrogantly. "I was getting a little flack about the way I was treating the articles so I decided to drop out and let them sweat for a while. They're beginning to come around to my way of thinking," he said smugly. "I've only been here two days and they've already passed anger and gone on to glorious panic." He grinned maliciously.

"But I thought the format was all set when you took the assignment?"

"They had an idea and a basic territory for me to cover, but the way I tied the articles together was up to me. At least I thought it was. All of a sudden they decided my pieces were too sensational, too depressing for a peace series. What they meant was they were too real. If they had wanted fairy tales they should have hired the Brothers Grimm," he finished in disgust.

"They won't try to get someone else, will they, Max? You know there are plenty of writers around who will give them just exactly what they want."

"I'm not worrying, Jiggs, so don't you either."

Max had a confidence in his own worth that she wished she had. As he talked quietly of the things he had seen in the tiny villages and crowded cities of the European countries he had visited, she realized what an enormously attractive man he was.

Why couldn't I have had an affair with Max instead of Matt? she wondered. They would have had a calmer, saner relationship and Max would have gentled her into the more disturbing human emotions, avoiding the drastic shock to her system that she had experienced with Matt.

Suddenly a curious thought struck her. Perhaps what she felt for Matt wasn't love after all. Perhaps possessiveness was a natural part of an affair of that intensity. Wouldn't she have felt the same about anyone who had given her the mind-boggling pleasure that Matt had?

But *could* anyone else have given her that much ecstasy? The thought came unbidden, adding to her confusion. Did she care for him because he gave her pleasure or did he give her pleasure because she cared for him? It was a tangle and she simply didn't have enough experience to know the answer.

Experience. She looked at Max out of the corner of her eye, seeing him only as a member of the opposite sex for the moment. Max was very attractive, sexy even. And—judging by the women she had seen wrapped around him at regular intervals during their association—very experienced. Would she feel desire if she kissed Max? Had her encounter with Matt unlocked her emotions enough for her to feel passion with someone else?

If it had, then it would mean that Matt had simply been a catalyst, releasing the passion she had suppressed for so long, and—having accomplished the release—he was no longer needed.

In hopeful desperation, she looked at Max's long, lean body. He was thin, but he looked very strong. He seemed a little pale, too. But maybe that was just his natural fairness. All in all, he wasn't bad—he just wasn't . . .

"Jiggs! Where the hell are you?"

She glanced up from his thin hands, so different from brown, rough, giant's hands, to see him staring at her with a genuinely puzzled look on his face. "I'm sorry, Max. I guess I was thinking of something else." As she apologized, her face went scarlet.

"I'd like to know what it was. You looked as though you were about to take some extremely nasty medicine."

"No, not nasty," she denied hastily, then realized how much she had admitted. "What I mean is . . . Oh, Max, I don't know what I mean. I'm so confused."

"Can I help?" he asked sincerely.

"That's what I'm asking myself and I just don't know." At his inquiring glance she continued, before she lost her nerve. "Max, I know you're always talking about my great body, but when you look at me, do you feel . . . well . . . lust?" She looked at him anxiously, waiting for his answer.

"Sugar, no man, no matter how old or infirm, could look at your body without feeling a little lust." He chuckled deeply and looked at her in amusement. "And I think I know where your tiny little mind is leading."

She glared at him, annoyed by his attitude. "Well, if you know so much, then why don't you help me out instead of letting me make a fool of myself?"

"Because it's your show, sugar. If I try to seduce you and fail, then I'll look like an ass. And if one of us has to look like an ass, I'd rather it were you."

"Some friend you are," she muttered indignantly, watching as he stretched out his legs comfortably, waiting. She moved her head slowly, wishing he would close his eyes or at least look away from her face. When she was an inch away from his lips, she jerked back, rising to pace the floor in agitation.

"I can't do it, Max." She shook her head in a violently negative movement. "I feel I'm being unfaithful. As though I'm breaking vows." Her voice rose in indignation. "Vows that I didn't make in the first place. I didn't promise anything, so why do I feel that I'm going back on my word?" She broke the rhythm of her stride to say in misery, "He probably doesn't care what I do, so why do I?"

Max looked at her for long moments with that strange analytical curiosity that she had seen in the past. When he spoke, his voice was quiet, thoughtful. "So you're still fighting it. I thought you had decided to stop running away."

"Damn it, Max! I admitted it was time for me to get my feet wet, but do I have to drown? Isn't there a happy medium?"

"No, Jiggs, there's not. You're either alive or you're dead. With no in-between. You were dead before and now you're alive. You can't choose the degree of emotion that you feel like you choose the shade of your lipstick. At least people as sensitive as you can't. You either feel with every bit of you or you don't feel at all. And until you realize that, Jiggs, and go with the current instead of fighting against it, you're going to make yourself a mountain of misery."

She flopped down beside him in disgust. "What am I going to do, Max? Do I just drop a lifetime of beliefs and go mindlessly where my emotions lead? That sounds so—so disorganized."

"Things are not always cut and dried, Jiggs. There are some things that are neither black nor white," he cautioned.

Max rose to his feet, his tall, lean figure casting a nebulous shadow in the dim light. He picked up the jacket he had discarded earlier and looked at the confusion written on her lovely face. "Only one more piece of advice from the old sage and then I'll leave. If you can never bring about a reconciliation between your slightly befuddled brain and your heart, go with the heart, honey. No hell on earth is worse than regretting a lost opportunity." He touched her softly on the cheek. "Just trust yourself, Jiggs. You're a very strong, very intelligent lady. You'll figure out what's right for you."

Jiggs walked to the door to see him out, a thousand thoughts ricocheting around inside her head. She didn't want Max to leave. He was familiar and comfortable and non-threatening. But she watched him walk to his car in silence. He had left her with new insights. More knots in the tangle. But he trusted her to untie those knots and she respected him enough at least to try.

As he drove away, she turned and reentered the late-afternoon gloom that filled the apartment. Staring at the shadows, his parting words returned to haunt her. What *was* right for her? She hated the thought of allowing her emotions to rule her mind. Everything she had seen in her observations of human relationships had reinforced the initial impression she had gained from her parents.

Thoughts of her parents flooded her mind. She

had always avoided thinking of her gentle, ineffective mother and her boisterous, untrustworthy father because with their images came the memory of pain.

Jiggs quickly crossed the living room and entered her bedroom, throwing off the bright caftan she was wearing and pulling on linen slacks and a light sweater. This was one thing she would stop hiding from right now. She hadn't been to visit her parents' graves in months and this time the visit would be more than a guilt-soothing duty trip. It was time she let go of the past, no matter how painful it was. Maybe then she could deal with the future.

As she laid the bunch of yellow and rust chrysanthemums between the two graves, she thought of her charming, deceiving father. He had such charm and he used it with a cunning that took one's breath away. Although he was third-generation Irish, he would lapse into a thick, strictly manufactured brogue in order to obtain what he wanted. It was usually a woman or a contract for his construction company that caused him to display his plumage, but occasionally he would turn on the brogue—and that charm—for Jiggs.

And she would always fall for it, a fact that had made her feel a traitor. But no matter how much she despised him for humiliating her mother, she had consistently succumbed. Later, of course, she had realized that he had needed his infrequent act as loving father to boost his ego. Everyone had to love Sean O'Malley.

And everyone had—including Jiggs. She had been just as hopelessly infatuated as her gentle mother. Only her mother had never seen, or she had pretended not to see, the dark side of Sean O'Malley. Jiggs had made one frustrating attempt to tell her of his affairs and of the way he ridiculed his adoring wife behind her back, but her mother had looked at her with those gentle, uncomprehending eyes and blithely ignored her warnings.

When Jiggs was seventeen her father had died in an automobile accident, leaving her with the double burden of caring for her distraught mother and coping with her own grief. She had watched her petite mother wither away—first mentally, then physically. Jiggs had known the grief-stricken woman was committing suicide in her own quiet way, but there had been nothing she could do to stop her. Her mother had died in her sleep eight heartbreakingly short months later.

Standing between the two graves, unaware of the soft, drizzling rain that was beginning to penetrate her clothing, Jiggs realized that not only had she never forgiven her father for *his* weakness, she had never forgiven her mother for hers. The contempt she had always felt for women who allowed men to ruin their lives had begun with her mother.

How could she have been so judgmental? What right did she have to think she was wise and to condemn others as wrong? She had been a child, seeing her parents with a child's eyes, understanding them with a child's reasoning. All these years she had avoided thinking about her parents, thinking about them as an adult. Although her parents' relationship had not been what she considered a healthy one, it was right for them. And they were the ones who mattered. They each had made a conscious choice. The depth of Jiggs's feelings for Matt had given her new insights into what motivated her gentle mother. Sean O'Malley had been the one person in the world who made her mother's life worthwhile. Imperfect as he was, he had given her happiness, had made her whole.

Jiggs straightened her back in determination. Silently, lovingly, she made her peace with the past and walked slowly to her parked car. While she was relieved that she could think now without bitterness of the two people who had given her life, her belief in her ideals—her judgment— had received another shattering blow. But at least she had taken a first step toward straightening out her tangled emotions. Perhaps the next step would be easier. She suddenly doubted it, though, because the next step was, of course, Matt. And she wasn't quite ready to think about Matt. She simply wanted to crawl into a dark hole and pray that when she crawled out again things would be back to normal—if she could call her life before Matt normal. Life before Matt. The words sounded like a historical marker. Life before electricity. Life before the smashing of the atom. Life before Matt.

Dear God, what was she going to do about Matt? She would have to call him tonight and explain, but what could she say that would sound rational? I'm sorry, Matt, but due to a sudden drop in the temperature of my feet, I won't be able to continue our affair? Or maybe—I can't see you again because I love you and it scares the hell out of me?

She recalled his reaction the last time she had shown doubts. He had been cold and distant and it would be much worse this time. Of course, that would make the ending of it much more final. And ending the affair was exactly what she wanted—wasn't it? So why was the thought tearing her apart?

What had he said that night? "Someday you'll find something that's worth risking a little of that sloppy emotion on." Sloppy was right. She felt like stopping the car and howling in pure misery.

But it was ridiculous to wallow in self-pity. It accomplished nothing. She needed to look at the situation logically.

Was loving Matt worth the risk? If she chose to end the affair she would be able to return to her uncomplicated, orderly life. Or would she? Even if she managed to cut the memory of Matt from her heart, hadn't she already seen how her eyes and mind had been opened to the world around her? No, there was no going back. Her life would be different. She would make friends—true friends like Max. She would have a fuller life because of Matt, but she wouldn't have Matt.

If she chose to continue the affair there was no guarantee that Matt wouldn't tire of her in a few months and drop her completely. Or that he wouldn't decide to try one of her father's tricks and juggle his women. She could be letting herself in for a lot of agony, but she would have Matt.

And that about summed it up. She could choose a better-rounded, fuller life without Matt—or a life that could possibly lead to even more misery with Matt.

Logically there was only one choice, but she simply couldn't bring herself to make it. Matt had given her more than any other human being and she couldn't forget that. Nor could she forget the love and laughter that existed for her only with Matt. She didn't want to end their affair. It was as simple as that. She wanted to live in his sunshine for as long as he would let her.

So finally the decision was made. Illogically, unreasonably. She would take what she could get from him for as long as she could get it. And if it included pain, she would take that too.

Positive that she had never made a more insane decision in her life, but totally unconcerned by the fact, she pulled into her parking space, then began to climb the stairs, wondering if she should drive back tonight or wait until tomorrow.

Tonight, she thought. I won't be able to sleep, so I might as well drive. But what am I going to say to him? After running out on him again how *can* I face Matt, she wondered, as she turned the corner to find herself facing Matt.

Ten

He stood still and straight in the middle of the railed walkway. Gone were the casual clothes she had come to accept as natural to him. His tan cord slacks and brown blazer accentuated his masculinity, but hid his enormous strength.

Jiggs stared hungrily at his face, devouring his craggy features with her eyes. She felt she had been separated from him for years. She wanted to touch him, reassure herself that he was real, but the look on his face held her back. It was a look totally different from any she had ever seen. This was much, much worse than she had anticipated. She had expected the cold, distant Matt—but not this total stranger.

She waited in silence for him to speak. Would Matt's voice come from this stranger's lips? Or would that be changed also? Apparently he wasn't going to give her a chance to find out, for the taut silence continued, stretching Jiggs's nerves to the breaking point.

Desperate to break the tension, she moved to unlock the door, her trembling fingers botching the simple procedure. She walked inside and fumbled for the light switch, watching anxiously as he entered the room behind her and glanced around.

His gaze touched on every piece of furniture, every painting, in the room as though seeing it all for the first time. Then his eyes returned to her and he began the same detached, but intimate, examination of her body.

His impersonal inspection seemed an obscene mockery of the affectionate looks she was used to receiving from him and it hurt unbearably. Had she thrown away the special relationship they had shared by giving rein to her insecurities? Had she destroyed whatever affection he had for her with her ridiculous doubts? The aching emptiness that followed the question caused her to shiver uncontrollably.

"Go change your clothes before you catch pneumonia."

It was his voice, yet it wasn't. There was no emotion in it. Not hurt nor hate. And certainly not affection. It was indescribably chilling. He was standing before one of her pen and ink drawings and had turned his head to look over his shoulder as he spoke. Looking again at the drawing, he seemed not to care whether or not she followed his curt advice.

Jiggs walked slowly to her bedroom, feeling a strange, debilitating weakness invade her body. Inside she leaned against the door, pain piercing her to the core. No sunshine for her now. He was so solemn, so strange.

A deep shuddering sigh shook her body, then she walked into the bathroom to change her clothes. She was through with running. She had

vowed to take what she could get from him and if
this was all he had to offer her, she would take it.
She had had a chance for more and she had
hesitated. Most people never find what she had
rejected. She deserved her punishment.

She stripped off her damp clothes and toweled
her hair dry as she walked naked back into the
bedroom, wondering how she was going to en-
dure his continued silence. It was all very well to
say she deserved his treatment, but she was very
much afraid she would scream in frustration if it
lasted much longer.

She felt Matt's presence, announced by that electrified current, moments before she saw him. He
was standing in the shadows of her bedroom,
staring at her body as she stood in the light streaming from the bathroom door. His inspection was
even more intimate than the one that had taken
place earlier—and this time his gaze was not detached. He searched out each vulnerable part of
her body, lingering with narrow-eyed greed on her
breasts, her flat stomach, the lush, gold, curling
triangle of hair that his hands and lips and body
had sought so much in the past days.

Memories of those moments flooded her body,
causing her nipples to harden into tight, firm
buds and her body to quiver in anticipation. She
ached with an all-consuming need—a burning,
frantic desire that caused her breath to come in
short, tremulous gasps.

Then he shifted slightly into the light and she
saw the expression in those narrowed eyes. Her
body had reacted to the loving memories, for there
was no loving affection in his look. There was
stark desire, but nothing of the gentleness re-
mained.

Frantic with fear, Jiggs searched the room desperately for an escape route—a place to hide her

vulnerability from his terrible eyes. She grabbed up the caftan she had discarded earlier and held it in front of her shivering nakedness.

As panicky thoughts ripped through her mind, she heard a strange sound—an ancient sound. The cry of an injured animal. Her head jerked up in alarm and saw his face seconds before he turned toward the door. Incredibly there had been a sheen of tears in his eyes and on his face was a look of ragged, undisguised pain.

"Matt!" she cried, halting his hurried steps. She walked softly to stand beside him, dropping the caftan to the floor. He turned his head slightly, not looking at her, but giving a subtle acknowledgement of her presence. "Matt," she said again, her voice gentle, loving.

Her tone released the breath he had been holding in a deep, shuddering sigh. He reached out to pull her body to his in a bruisingly tight embrace. Grasping her hair with one hand, he pulled her head from his shoulder painfully and crushed her lips in a kiss that devoured.

He was totally out of control, his movements demanding, as he pulled her across the room to the bed and discarded his clothes. Pushing her back onto the bed, he threw himself on her, his need critical. The fierceness with which he touched her body contained an unconcealed desperation, which was transmitted to Jiggs and her responses took on an urgent insistence. This was no gentle loving. This was burning, compelling necessity. A rough kind of magic that took them quickly to an explosive, shuddering release.

Afterward, she had no idea whether she had lost consciousness or if she had simply fallen asleep from exhaustion. When she awoke she was in the bed alone and she lay quietly in the dark, thinking of the wild mating that had just taken place.

She could feel the bruises on her body and knew her nails had left deep scratches on his back. The barely contained violence of his lovemaking held no terrors for her. She could meet his needs with needs of her own. But the desperation behind it baffled her. It was as though he had needed the violence to imprint their lovemaking indelibly in his mind—as though it were the last time!

She jumped from the bed, pulled on the caftan and ran from the room, terrified at the thought which became stronger with each passing moment. She had to find him and reassure herself that her impression had been wrong.

The living room and kitchen were empty. She leaned her head against the front door and felt the strength drain from her body, in despair. It was several long minutes later before the faint sounds of movement in her studio penetrated her misery.

She flew down the hall, wiping the tears from her face, and opened the door. She stopped just inside as he turned his head away from his quiet contemplation of the watercolors, which covered every inch of wall space.

"You have a great talent, Jiggs." His voice was quiet, unutterably weary.

"Thank you." What could she say to him? How could she break through the barriers he had erected? "Matt, I'd like to explain."

"Why do you hide them in here?"

He was not going to let her explain or apologize for running away. She lifted her head in determination. If he wouldn't let her explain in her own way, then she would go along with him. But one way or another she would get her point across.

"I told myself that I wasn't ready for a showing. I told myself that I couldn't let strangers see the inside of my head by looking at my paintings. I told myself everything except the truth. I was afraid, Matt. Afraid to take a chance on failing."

She walked to stand beside him and looked at the painting on the wall before him. "This one was painted just after my mother's death," she explained quietly.

"I thought watercolors were supposed to be gentle and soft," he mused. "How did you manage to express such violence with so few strokes?"

"All my anger and frustration went into that painting," she recalled. "I thought at the time it expressed a kind of civilized rage, but I see now that it was merely repressed like all my other emotions." She looked at his face, but he continued to stare at the painting and with a sigh of resignation she continued. "I watched my mother die, Matt. She slowly, intentionally gave up her life right before my eyes and no matter how I tried, I couldn't do a damn thing to stop her. I failed. That was when I began to live my life so that failure of that magnitude could never touch me again."

At last, Matt turned to face her. "I'm sorry, Jiggs. About your mother, but also for what just happened." He closed his eyes as though in terrible pain. "God, baby, I'm so sorry. That was not why I followed you here. God knows I needed it, but I never meant to hurt you." He looked at her closely, then gently touched the bruise on the side of her neck. "And I did hurt you, didn't I?"

Before she could deny his words, he continued to speak. "I came here to apologize. I didn't mean to compound my guilt by practically raping you." He ignored her protest. "Jiggs, I saw the terror in your eyes in there. I never thought I'd see that look in your eyes. Anger or disgust maybe, but not terror."

He paused, walking a few feet away, before turning abruptly to face her. "I came here to tell you that the whole mess was my fault. I knew you would feel guilty for running away again, but I wanted you to know that I understood." He took a deep breath, as though he had to force himself to continue. "Jiggs, I cheated. I knew you had doubts about our relationship, but I ignored them and pushed you—blackmailed you—into going to bed with me."

She stared at him in confusion. What was he talking about? He was carrying an enormous load of guilt over something. "But, Matt—"

"Jiggs, wait. Let's go sit down so that I can explain it to you. I want you to know the truth."

She followed him into the living room and sat on the loveseat, facing him solemnly as he took the large armchair. He stared for a while into space as though gathering his words and, incredibly, it seemed, his courage.

"Do you remember the night you told me how important my friendship was to you?" She nodded, waiting. "I believed you. I could see that you honestly valued my friendship. And I took advantage of that fact. I hoped that you would fight to keep it. So," he sighed deeply and looked straight into her eyes, "I deliberately withheld my friendship in order to force you into a decision that you weren't ready to make."

"Matt, please listen to me," Jiggs said earnestly, hating the self-blame she saw in his eyes. "There was one reason and one reason only why I slept with you that first night—pure, unadulterated lust. I'll admit that I considered coming to you after you turned cold and distant, but that night—that glorious night, Matt! That had nothing to do with friendship. Later, of course, the two were inextricably intertwined, but the night I met you in the hall I wasn't looking for friendship. I had been unable to sleep because I needed you so badly." She looked at him with smiling indulgence. "And don't tell me you arranged that because I won't believe you."

"Of course, I didn't. I had been thinking of nothing but you for three days straight. When you appeared in the hall it was as though my need had conjured you up. I was afraid if I moved you would disappear," he murmured, caught up in the memory. Then he leaned forward and said urgently, "But, Jiggs, don't you understand? Even if you didn't realize it, even if it made no difference—I cheated on our agreement."

She couldn't allow him to continue feeling guilt over what she considered a very human error. He had worked to bring about something that was important to him—by slightly devious means it was true, but he meant no mental or physical harm to her. He was not a man to sit back and wait for things to happen. He took the bull by the horns and *made* them happen.

She looked at him sternly. "So Mr. Perfect finally made a mistake," she scoffed gently. "Big dumb deal. It simply means I don't have to worry so much about all the mistakes I make. I don't know if I've mentioned it," she said in a confidential tone, "but I can't heat milk."

Matt stared at her silently, his strong face thoughtful, then began to chuckle. "I guess that means you forgive me." He looked at the loving amusement showing in her face. "I don't deserve it, Jiggs, especially after tonight, but thank you."

She stood and moved across to his chair, kneeling before him, feeling the need to touch him. There was one more ghost that she had to lay to rest before they moved on to other, more pleasant diversions. "About tonight, Matt." She held his face with one hand to keep him from turning away in self-disgust and looked deeply into his dark eyes. "Listen to me, love. You're not looking logically at what we shared tonight. And I did say *shared*, Matt. If you'll check your back you'll see that I'm not the ravaged—I was the ravager, too. Yes, I did quite a bit of ravaging myself. I have never in my life experienced anything like that. You pulled something from deep inside me that I didn't even know existed. It was something so exciting and so special, I'll never forget it as long as I live." She caressed his face softly, trying to find the right words. "The circumstances that brought about what happened tonight will never occur again . . . I hope. Which means the consequences—that special joining, that intensity, that depth of feeling we shared—was a once in a lifetime event. And that makes it even more precious. Something to pull out of my store of memories on a cold night. What I'm trying to say in my own clumsy way is—I loved it, Matt. Every glorious minute of it."

His eyes were shining suspiciously as he turned his head to give her hand a soft, almost worshipful kiss, then he said simply, "Thank you."

"You're very welcome, believe me. Now not another word about it," she ordered. As she was struck by a thought, she laughed in mischievous amusement, earning an inquiring glance from Matt. "Darling, Max would have a field day analyzing you."

He raised his gentle giant's hand to her head, stroking her auburn hair and sighing in contentment as she rested her head on his knee. Then with quiet curiosity, "What made you think of Max?"

"Max loves what he calls 'people watching.' He picks us mortals to pieces with his fiendish little brain, never satisfied until he finds out what makes us tick. Then he puts us into convenient categories. I bet he would have to invent a new category for you." She chuckled. "I remember thinking when he was here this afternoon that—"

"He was here? In your apartment?" His voice sounded curiously stiff. "I thought he was in Europe."

Jiggs looked at him sharply, perplexed by his disgruntled tone. "Yes, he was, but he came back because—Matt, what's wrong?"

He stood abruptly and her derrière met the floor with a hard thud. She rose slowly, rubbing her injured posterior, and watched totally bewildered, as he paced back and forth in agitation.

"Why in the hell did he come here, Jiggs?" He looked at her, accusation in his eyes. "He's a friend, too, isn't he, Jiggs? I asked you once the first day I met you and I'll ask you again—how good a friend is he?"

"Now wait just a minute, Matt. You have no right to question me in that tone." She glared at him furiously. "You have no right to question me at all!"

"I'll question you at any time, in any tone I damn well please!" he shouted, grabbing her arm. His face was red with rage. "Now you had better tell me what happened here this afternoon before I give you the shaking of your life. You were upset and your *good friend*, Max, just happened to show up," he fumed. "So then what happened?"

"You great, hulking oaf! You'll shake me with the help of the Marines!" She jerked her arm from his grasp. "Nothing happened!"

Never in her life had she been so furious. The absolute nerve of the man! As if she would—

She stopped rubbing her arm, suddenly remembering. She had tried to see if Max could help her forget Matt. And although she couldn't bring herself to touch him, she *had* tried.

"Jiggs," he said, his voice suspicious. "Jiggs, I see guilt in your face."

She turned to walk away from him, but he pulled her back. "Jiggs, that's guilt and don't you deny it!"

She sighed and faced him in resignation. "Matt, it was nothing really. I simply wanted to see if he could—" She stopped abruptly, her eyes widening in wonder. "Matt, you're *jealous*!"

"Jiggs," he warned through clenched teeth. "Don't you dare try to change the subject. You wanted to see if Max could do what, for heaven's sake?"

"Forget Max for a minute," she said in urgent excitement. "Today I was trying to figure something out. I haven't had enough experience to know, but you have. If you feel jealous and possessive, does that mean you're in love?"

He closed his eyes in frustration, then opened them to look at her as he quietly answered her question. "Those things alone don't mean love, but when they're added to—to loving friendship, then, yes, it does mean you're in love." He framed her face gently with his large hands. "And if you're trying to ask if all that shouting means I love you, then—even though it's a very poor way of showing it—I do. More than I ever thought possible, Jiggs." His hands tightened on her face. "Now, please, *please*, finish that damned sentence. You wanted to see if Max could *what*?"

She put her arms around his waist and squeezed him in exuberant joy. "You darling, darling man! I wanted to see if Max could help me forget you. But, Matt," she continued as she felt his body jerk. "I couldn't touch him. I looked him over and decided he was very sexy, but he wasn't you." She laughed, delighted at her good taste. "I couldn't go through with it because I love you. I felt I was being unfaithful even to try."

"And you were right!" he said huffily. "Sexy! What in hell's that supposed to mean?"

His voice was filled with disgust, causing Jiggs to chuckle in indulgent amusement. She backed away to look at his face, loving every rugged, annoyed line. Then his face froze and moments later he jerked her to his chest, her breath leaving her lungs in a soft whoosh as she made hard contact with his chest.

"Jiggs! You said you love me," he whispered, his voice trembling slightly with emotion.

"Yes, darling," she gasped, her voice weak and restricted from the tight embrace. "And if you'll let me breathe," she panted, "I'll show you how much."

"God, sweetheart! I'm sorry," he apologized, loosening his grip and watching as she took a deep breath. "Jiggs, your face is bright red." His voice held puzzled concern.

"Yes, darling," she said, patting his arm. "That's what happens when you cut off a person's oxygen. But don't worry about it. I had planned on cutting down anyway." She touched his bemused face in wonder. "Besides I know exactly how you feel. I want to shout or run or *something*!"

He laughed delightedly, throwing back his head and whirling her around in a movement of pure joy. He dropped into the chair with Jiggs in his arms. "That's how I felt when you woke up that very first morning. I didn't recognize it as love then, but I knew I wanted you—a stranger—more than I had ever wanted anything in my life. There was something special between us from that first moment. When you ran out I thought it was some evil fate working—letting me have a glimpse of happiness, then taking it away." He closed his eyes, remembering. "When Sam showed me your application, I couldn't believe my luck. Yours was too unusual a name for it to be coincidence, but I checked with Sam to be sure." He chuckled softly. "You were lost before you ever set foot in my office, darlin'. I was determined not to let you get away a second time. It wasn't until I saw you in my home that I knew I really loved you. You looked so right there. It was as though I had unconsciously designed the house with you in mind." He shuddered as a painful memory flitted through his mind. "I thought I had lost you through my own stupidity. You kept talking about friendship when I desperately wanted your love. I was afraid I had rushed you into something you weren't ready for and as a result you ran." He looked at her with sharp, narrowed eyes. "Why did you run, Jiggs?"

She opened her mouth to put him off, but stopped in time. She owed him the truth. "I found out I was jealous, Matt. Agonizingly, possessively jealous. I heard you talking to Barbie on the phone and I wanted to rip that phone right out of your hand! The power of my emotions scared me—then."

He stared at her in amazement. "Barbie? Why should you be jealous of Barbie?"

"Why should you be jealous of Max?" she countered.

"Oh, I see what you mean. But, darlin', I haven't seen Barbie since long before the night I met you."

"Matt, you don't have to explain," she said, meaning every word. "I trust you."

"But I want to. Barbie's a nice lady and we owe her a lot. If she hadn't had a migraine and stood me up—and if you hadn't had a crush on Lincoln—you and I would probably never have met." His hold tightened at the thought. "Barbie and I were lovers, Jiggs. Lovers who decided to be friends instead. It's as simple as that. Nobody could ever give me what you do, Jiggs. Don't ever doubt that."

She looked into his beautiful face, love shining from her eyes. "I won't, Matt. No more doubts—ever. I made my choice once and for all today." She kissed him gently, quivering as she felt his blazing response.

Drawing away slowly from the kiss, he whispered huskily, "It's been a long day, sweet. Don't you think it's time for bed?"

She smiled contentedly and laid her head on his shoulder. "Matthew Brady, you've got a one-track mind." She closed her eyes with a smug sigh. "Isn't it wonderful that mine runs on the same track?"

Laughing as he stood with her in his arms, he said, "and you, Jiggs O'Malley . . ." He paused, looking down at her. "Darlin', what in the hell is your real name?"

"Jiggs O'Malley," she said innocently.

"Jiggs," he reproved. "That isn't your real name and you know it. Your job application showed the initials 'J.I.' in parentheses."

"You don't need to know." Her face was set in stubborn lines.

"You hard-headed mule, they'll want to know when we apply for a marriage license."

"Oh." She looked at him, startled. "Are we getting married, Matt? That's wonderful!"

He sighed in exasperation. "Darlin', sometimes you're so dense. Of course we're getting married." He looked at her sharply. "That is what you want, isn't it?"

"Oh yes, Matt! More than anything—now that I think about it. I hadn't planned that far ahead. I had only thought as far as loving you," she explained.

"Well, hold that thought!" He laughed. "But right now I want to know your real name."

"All right, all right," she muttered, then set her jaw, her eyes daring him to laugh. "Jessamine Iona O'Malley."

She watched as he struggled to control his features. He swallowed loudly, took a deep breath and said, "I think it's time for bed, *Jiggs.*"

Her laughter echoed behind them as he carried her into the bedroom and slammed the door shut with his foot.

Two months later Jiggs and Matt were driving along a dusty road, catching glimpses of a winding river through bare trees, headed for home. As glorious as their sunshine-filled honeymoon had been, they were both anxious to return to the warmth of home for Christmas.

Matt, deliberately teasing, slowed the car just before they rounded the bend that would give them their first view of the house.

"You fiend," she cried, laughing.

"Anyone who sings 'Kill da' wabbit' to the music of 'The Ride of the Valkyries,' for *two hundred miles,*" he said righteously, "deserves all the punishment she can get."

"Can I help it if I'm addicted to Bugs Bunny cartoons?" she asked, fluttering her eyelashes. "Besides if you didn't like it you should have put on a different tape. Now drive faster."

Chuckling in delight at her excited anticipation, he drove faster and minutes later they pulled into the drive. They sat for quiet moments, staring contentedly. Then Matt turned and kissed her gently. "Welcome home, darlin'."

He had said the same words two months earlier as he held her tightly in the darkened bedroom of her apartment. Now the words had a different, but equally loving, meaning. Her smile echoed his pleasure in their return.

"Come on, Mrs. Brady. I want to see Saul and Ruth," he said, grabbing her hand and pulling her across the seat.

She rolled her eyes and sighed as she was hauled from the car. "Matt, darling, there's something I've been meaning to talk to you about."

He stopped and turned to look at her. "What is it, Jiggs?"

But she didn't get the chance to make the complaint, for Ruth and Saul emerged from the house at that moment. Oh, well, she mused silently, giving Matt a lovingly indulgent look, he'll probably realize the effect of all that pulling when my left hand begins to drag on the ground. She turned to embrace the laughing pair and followed them into the house.

As they sat in front of the crackling fire later that evening, the twinkling lights of the huge Christmas tree made their homecoming perfect. They had added their gifts for Ruth and Saul to the pile already under the tree, but Jiggs had her gifts for Matt hidden away. She refused to let him open them before Christmas and she had already caught him tampering with them once. She had wanted to buy him everything in sight; however she kept her purchases simple. Her favorite was of her own making—a watercolor she had done on their honeymoon. It showed a figure, vaguely resembling herself, trapped in a dark forest of dead trees with gnarled, grasping branches. On the left side of the painting, glorious sunlight was streaming through the trees as the figure stared at it with wondrous longing.

She suddenly wished she had not been so stubborn about waiting until Christmas morning to open the gifts. She wanted to give the watercolor to Matt now. She wanted to see his face when he understood what she was telling him. And she didn't doubt for a minute that he would understand. She knew him too well.

Saul entered the room and gave Matt a very mysterious nod. Matt smiled broadly at the conspiratorial signal, turning to her to echo her wish.

"Jiggs, I've got a gift for you in the bedroom and I don't want to wait until Christmas to give it to you. We can call it a welcome home gift."

She looked at him, puzzled by his suppressed excitement and unmistakable amusement. What was he planning? She didn't trust him when he got that look in his eyes. "Matt, what are you up to? If you've got something outrageous in the bedroom, you'd better tell me now or, so help me, you'll be sorry."

"Darlin'!" he said in an injured tone. "Would I do that to you?"

"Yes, you would," she stated unequivocally.

"I promise it's nothing outrageous—just a little portrait."

She looked at him suspiciously. "A portrait of whom?"

"Patience, darlin'," he said grinning. "Come and see."

Curiosity piqued, she followed closely as he left the room. Outside their bedroom door he stopped and demanded she close her eyes.

"Matt, is that absolutely necessary?"

"Humor me. Come on, Jiggs. I don't want you to see it until you're standing in front of it."

She closed her eyes impatiently and let him lead her into the room. He pulled her to a halt, positioning her while she grumbled irritably, then said, "Okay, open them."

She carefully opened her eyes to look at the

portrait before her. For a few seconds she simply stared in open-mouthed surprise. Then as she took in the lean cheeks, familiar beard, and famous stovepipe hat of the man in the portrait, her delighted peal of laughter filled the room.

"Oh, Matt," she gasped. "It's perfect."

He pulled her into his arms and whispered, "*It's* appropriate. *You're* perfect."

His kiss was a tribute to their joy in each other and as it deepened, the eyes of the great man in the portrait on the wall seemed to twinkle in approval of their loving union.

THE EDITOR'S CORNER

Delightful. Good old Webster says that delightful describes "That which gives keen lively pleasure to mind, heart, senses." So, there was no other word I could possibly use to sum up how your reception of *LOVESWEPT* has made all of us who work on the series feel. Your warm, enthusiastic notes and letters, along with the generous remarks of reviewers, have been truly *delightful!* Our authors join me in thanking you for the keen lively pleasure that your response has given us.

Next month's *LOVESWEPT* romances reflect the brilliance of the July days when you'll be reading them. They shimmer with emotion, sizzle with romance! All three authors live in sun-drenched California. What a coincidence—or is it?

HARD DRIVIN' MAN (#10) by Nancy Carlson doesn't have just the hero in the driver's seat of an 18-wheeler, but also the young and lively heroine. And a more feminine truck-driver heroine you can't imagine. This is a fiery and truly exciting romance . . . and how it made its way into my hands may interest you. A little over a year ago I gave a workshop for prospective *LOVESWEPT* authors in southern California. Emphasizing that fresh elements were essential in our love stories, I mentioned that, for example, no one had ever sent me a romance featuring truck drivers. Further, I commented that I'd read an article about several charming women who are successful in this job. Well, about a week after I got back to my office, **HARD DRIVIN' MAN** arrived in the mail with a note from Nancy's agent clipped to it. The note read, "Ask and you shall receive!" Now, I wonder, what other marvelous

(continued)

areas are being neglected because I haven't thought of them and asked? I'd love to hear from you about occupations, settings, and so forth that you feel are bypassed and you would like to see in our romances.

BELOVED INTRUDER (#11) is in the tradition of Noelle Berry McCue's highly popular love stories! It is a romance of searing and intense emotion, incendiary passion. I can't tell you how much respect and affection I have for Noelle. This novel was created during a period of great stress for her because of illness in the family. Not only did she come through with a riveting book, but she came through on schedule. She's a real pro and a lady with real courage.

We are sincerely pleased to be able to publish Joan J. Domning's first book, **HUNTER'S PAYNE** (#12). There is a matchless incandescence of feeling in this romance. As editor I go over a *LOVESWEPT* romance at least four times, the last in the galley or proof stage. And, even the fourth time through, I chuckled and despaired with Karen Hunter and P. Lee Payne . . . and believe I could never fail to respond to their moving scene on pages 177 and 178!

Happy July reading with *LOVESWEPT*!

Carolyn Nichols

Carolyn Nichols
  Editor
LOVESWEPT
Bantam Books, Inc.
666 Fifth Avenue
New York, NY 10103